Kate had to run hard to keep up with a guy like Ross. . . .

By the time she reached the orange grove, he was waiting for her, a big grin on his face.

"So you finally made it," he teased.

"It wasn't a fair race. You're a track star," she panted.

"No alibis. You lost, you have to pay the price."

"What price?"

"This."

He caught her by the shoulders and pressed a kiss on her lips. She was surprised, but didn't move her head away. Her mouth was soft and receptive—yes, she wanted to kiss him.

Dear Reader,

At Silhouette we publish books with you in mind. We're pleased to announce the creation of Silhouette First Love, a new line of contemporary romances written by the finest young-adult writers as well as outstanding new authors in this field.

Silhouette First Love captures many of the same elements enjoyed by Silhouette Romance readers—love stories, happy endings and the same attention to detail and description. But First Love features young heroines and heroes in contemporary and recognizable situations.

You play an important part in our future plans for First Love. We welcome any suggestions or comments on our books and I invite you to write to us at the address below.

Karen Solem
Editor-in-Chief
Silhouette Books
P.O. Box 769
New York, N.Y. 10019

KATE HERSELF
Helen Erskine

First Love from Silhouette

Published by Silhouette Books New York

America's Publisher of Contemporary Romance

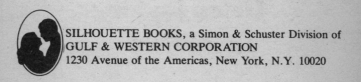

SILHOUETTE BOOKS, a Simon & Schuster Division of
GULF & WESTERN CORPORATION
1230 Avenue of the Americas, New York, N.Y. 10020

ISBN: 0-671-53306-1

First Silhouette Books printing October, 1981

10 9 8 7 6 5 4 3 2 1

KATE
HERSELF

1

Kate looked at Ross, then over her shoulder to be sure he was talking to her. It would be just like her to gush, "I'd love to go to a movie Friday night!" then have one of the pretty, popular girls step forward to accept the invitation . . . or reject it. Incredibly, there were one or two girls in Orange Grove High who were capable of turning down a date with Ross Barrows— Lela Granger, for example.

Lela was not behind her. Neither was any other girl. She and Ross were alone in the school library, except for a teacher who sat at a desk some distance away.

"A movie?" she said.

She still wasn't sure there was not some mistake. She'd hoped for a miracle with the beginning of her junior year—that she'd somehow attract the attention of a really exciting boy. But could it have happened so soon, the second week of school? Maybe he'd said that *he* was going to a movie Friday night, and her imagination had done the rest. Her fantasies could be very real. Had he actually said, "Would you like to go to a movie Friday night?"

He pushed at the thicket of rust-colored hair that tumbled over his forehead, shifted his feet with a hint of impatience.

"I suggested a movie," he said, "but if there's something you'd rather do—"

She wasn't dreaming. Ross Barrows, one of the best-looking, most popular boys in school—*a senior*—had asked her out.

"Oh, no, a movie is fine," she said. "There's nothing I'd rather do. I've been a movie fan all my life. I—" She'd started to say she'd go to a movie every night if her parents would let her, but by clamping her jaws together she'd managed to bring her babbling to a halt.

He smiled, teeth white against his sun-bronzed skin, the hint of impatience gone.

"I'm a pretty rabid fan myself," he said. "Oh, you'd better give me your address in case I don't see you before Friday."

His voice was as deep as her father's. He was man-sized, too, at least six feet tall with wide shoulders and the rest of him lean as a whippet. His features were large and cleanly chiseled, with only the dark-blue eyes, very clear and direct as a child's, to suggest the boy he had been only a few years before . . . oh, yes, and a few freckles sprinkled across the straight nose.

"Of course," she said. She fumbled with her notebook, tore out a sheet of paper, and in the process dropped her pen. He picked it up, and handed it to her. As she wrote her address she hoped he didn't notice how her hand shook.

He looked at the slip of paper, folded it, and tucked it into the pocket of his green knit polo shirt. The pocket had the famous Gucci stripes.

"Will seven-thirty be all right?" he said. "If you're

anything like I am you like to catch a movie from the beginning."

She'd been acting like a ninny, babbling, dropping things, getting flushed and breathless as if she'd never talked to a boy before. Even if you feel like a nerd you don't have to act like one, she scolded herself. And raising her head, she spoke quite airily.

"Seven-thirty would be fine. See you then."

She stepped around him and walked down the hall, wondering if he was looking after her. If he was, she thought, he was seeing a girl who was neither tall nor short, plump or slender, blonde or brunette—an in-between girl who was average in every way. If there was anything that made her look at all different it was the combination of her gray eyes and dark hair. Wouldn't you know that she hadn't taken after either of her folks, but had inherited her hair from her father, her eyes from her mother? Her eyes were nice, though, wide with thick dark lashes—by far her best feature. He couldn't see them now, of course. Yet he had seen them, while they'd sat across from each other in the library. Was it her eyes that had made him decide to ask her for a date?

She gave up trying to take notes in social studies, or even to listen, as she lived over the last eventful hour. She'd gobbled a quick lunch at noon, eating out in the yard with Doris. Then she'd hurried to the library to do some research for an English essay. She'd pulled a half-dozen books from the shelves, taken a seat, and had just spread the books out around her when Ross Barrows had come into the library. He sat down across from her, and opened a chemistry book, not glancing at her, or any of the kids at the table. Ross was a senior, but even if they'd been fellow classmates, Kate wasn't silly enough to think he'd notice her. He was one of the top boys in school, one of the kids that made things happen at Orange Grove High. He even played drums in a trio that had played a few professional gigs.

She was Kate Fleming. Not Katherine. Just plain Kate. When she was ten she'd decided to use her full name Katherine—had insisted on it until her mother told her in the gentle but too-patient tone she so often used with her, "Katherine is not your name, dear. You were christened Kate. Just plain Kate."

Still, a cat can look at a king, and so she stole an occasional glance across the library table, under the protection of her fanlike lashes. Ross was frowning over the chemistry book, and now and then he'd run a hand through his thick hair in a gesture of frustration. She'd thought that if life was like the movies he'd look up suddenly, give her an appealing grin and say, "You don't happen to know anything about chemistry, do you?"

And she'd reply quietly, "Why, yes, that happens to be my favorite subject. I'd be happy to coach you. Why don't you come to my house this evening?"

Life was not like the movies. He continued to frown over the textbook, and she continued to steal glances at the scowling but still handsome features.

Finally, when the noon hour was almost over, and they were the only ones left in the library, except for the teacher, he'd looked across the table at the exact moment she'd stolen a glance at him. His face had lit up in such a friendly smile that her embarrassment died away.

"You're one of the Fleming sisters, aren't you?" he said.

"The middle one." Her voice was surprisingly matter-of-fact. She was on very familiar ground, discussing the fact she was one of the three Fleming sisters, the middle one whose first name no one remembered.

"I know Anne," he said, his smile warm now. "She was always a class ahead of me, but I thought she was great, always so nice to everyone."

Kate gave the smile that any reference to Anne called for—gracious, a bit grave, like Anne, herself. Anne the Good.

"And you have a sister who's a lower classman, don't you?" he said. "Carrie?"

That called for a grin. "Yes, she's a freshman."

He nodded. "I'm with a combo, and we were looking for a girl singer the first week of school. Carrie heard about it and wanted to try out. We hated to tell her she was too young. She can sing, and she's as cute as—"

"As a kitten." Cute, adorable Carrie.

"Yes." He grinned at the memory of fourteen-year-old Carrie, then his features straightened. "And you're—?"

"Kate."

"Kate. Umm." He looked at her and gave a little nod as if to say the name fit her. Then he said, "Do you sing, Kate?"

"Heavens, no!" She could have added, I don't do much of anything except maintain a B average in school, and do the chores at home that Anne's too old for, and Carrie's too young for. Of course she didn't. Even to her own ears the words would have sounded self-pitying.

"I'm sorry," he said. Then added, "Oh, I'm Ross. Ross Barrows."

She had to laugh. "That's who I thought you were. Ross Barrows, vice president of the senior class, track star, musician—I could go on and on."

"Please don't," he said, flushing with becoming

modesty. Then he said almost coaxingly, "You're sure you don't sing?"

"Very sure. Anne sings like an angel. Carrie sings like a fourteen-year-old Linda Ronstadt. But I, Kate, do not sing."

He looked at her, one rust-colored brow cocked quizzically, as if he thought there was more to what she said than the words. Then, abruptly, he gave up trying to solve the puzzle, and pushed back his chair.

It was over, and she wouldn't try to prolong it. She would not be one of those pathetic girls who tried to attach herself to a boy because he'd spoken a few casual words to her. In her determination not to let him guess that this brief encounter had given her material for endless hours of daydreaming, she became Anne. Sweet, gracious, slightly remote in her dignity. It was a personality she could easily slip in to. A little nod, a benevolent smile, and she gathered up the library books. Without displaying undue haste, which would have been out of character for her older sister, she managed to get away from the table before Ross did.

Once she was in the stacks, the mantle of calm composure deserted her. Her brain, eyes and hands, were out of sync. She couldn't seem to find where the books belonged, and when she did she dropped one, trying to wedge it into its proper place. When she'd picked it up, and squeezed it in among its fellows, she started to the door . . . only to find Ross standing there, apparently waiting for her.

She hesitated, wanting to avoid another encounter with him, afraid she'd make a fool of herself if she had another chance. Then the bell rang, and she started forward. If he continued to stand there, blocking the door, she'd make a joke of it. She'd be Carrie, Cute

Carrie, wrinkling her nose, smiling impishly. *"Excuse meeee—"* she'd say, doing her younger sister's Steve Martin imitation.

But he spoke first. "Would you like to go to a movie Friday night?" he said.

That was when she'd looked over her shoulder, certain that one of Orange Grove's prettiest girls must have come out from the stacks. And when she'd realized she was the one he'd asked out she'd babbled, and made a fool of herself. But not completely. At the end, she'd got herself together and acted—not with the dignity of Anne, not with the pixie cuteness of Carrie, but with her own middling sort of cool. "Seven-thirty would be fine. See you then."

So far, so good. But now what? How could she handle a date with Ross Barrows when her only dating experience had been with Jeff Carlson, a neighborhood boy she'd known all her life? Even going out with him on her first date had been a disaster, with her hand so sweaty when he'd reached for it in the movie that he'd promptly let it go, and wiped his hand on his handkerchief. Later, laughing at one of his whispered jokes, she'd choked on a piece of popcorn, and created a horrible disturbance, some people loudly shushing her, while others tried to give her first aid.

"Boy, I'm glad that's over," Jeff had muttered when a glass of water the usher brought had mercifully cleared her windpipe.

Nothing like that must happen Friday night with Ross. She wouldn't eat popcorn, and she'd put antiperspirant on her hands. Of course there were a hundred other ways she could turn the evening into a shambles. She wasn't sure she'd outgrown the giggles. What if the picture was a comedy and she started laughing and couldn't stop?

Maybe she'd ask Anne for some pointers. But she knew what Anne would say. "Just be yourself, Kate." *I would be if I knew who I was.*

Maybe Carrie would have some new jokes she could pull on Ross. Only she wasn't good at telling jokes. Even if she remembered the punch line the funniest story fell flat when she told it.

Kate usually rode the bus home, but today she decided to walk. It was three miles, but it was a perfect September day, with only a bit of smog in the air which had to be expected when there was no wind to blow it out of the valley.

Orange Grove was something like Kate, she often thought. It wasn't a big city, nor was it a small town, but something in between. It was also between two big, famous cities, Los Angeles to the north, San Diego to the south. It did have a distinctive feature, though, much as she had her gray eyes and dark hair. Any resident of Orange Grove would tell you it had the most equable climate in the country, sheltered as it was by the mountain range that almost surrounded it.

Sometimes Kate thought it would be fun to live where there were four distinct seasons, but not today. Today she could have no regrets about anything. Orange Grove, California, was the only place in the world to be. As she strolled along, daydreaming, her self-doubts eased. So she wasn't lovely and poised like Anne, or cute like Carrie. She must have something or Ross wouldn't have asked her out.

A car rattled up and stopped beside her. Jeff Carlson stuck his head out the window. "Going my way?" Greenish eyes with white lashes and brows peered from under a shock of corn-colored hair that fell over his face, giving him the look of a sheep dog. All at once she saw him for what he was—a skinny kid with an unfinished look about his features. She marveled that she'd ever been so nervous on a date with him that she'd sweated, and choked on a piece of popcorn.

She waved him on, in a not unkindly gesture. "Thanks. I'm walking for my health."

"Aw, come on." He'd been sixteen for only a month, and was so proud of the old clunker he'd sunk his life savings in that it was pathetic. Still, she shook her head, and again waved him on.

"Okay, walk!" he yelled, like an aggrieved child, and rattled off.

She went back to thinking of Ross, wondering how she could possibly handle a date with him, why he'd asked her out, anyway. Was it an impulse that he already regretted? Or did he think that because she was so ordinary he could take liberties with her he couldn't take with a girl like Lela Granger? Boys had to get their experience somehow, and she'd read that they sometimes went with plain girls for that reason, like doctors getting their medical experience treating the poor.

She was borrowing trouble, a habit of hers—when she wasn't going to the opposite extreme and concocting happy-ever-after fairy tales. . . .

She slowed her steps, not anxious to get home. Her favorite fairy tale was more real now than it had ever been, and she became so immersed in it that she was barely aware of the familiar landmarks along the way, trees, and houses—the cracks in the pavement, and the uneven curbs. Prince Charming was running a hand through his hair, and smiling at her, dark-blue eyes gazing deeply into her eyes, when she tripped over the worst curb along the way, and nearly fell.

By the time she'd righted herself the prince was speaking. "There's a ball at the palace Friday night. I'll come for you in the royal carriage. Will seven-thirty be all right?"

The scenario was still unreeling in her mind when she reached the front door of the ranch-style home she'd lived in most of her life. There reality returned. What would her mother's greeting be today? There were three possibilities. One—"Change your clothes before you do anything else." Two—"Don't change your clothes. I want you to run some errands for me." Then there was the always popular, "If you've got homework to do, do it now. Later you'll want to watch television."

Whatever the order of the day happened to be, her mother would catch herself after a minute, give her a somewhat weary smile and say, "How was your day, dear?"

How was your day, Mom? she sometimes thought. How is your life? Has it been worthwhile for you, never doing anything but taking care of Dad and your three girls? Yet she'd always been secretly pleased that her mother had never had an outside job.

Remembering not to slam the door she called out, "I'm home, Mom!"

Her mother stepped out of the kitchen, drying her hands on her apron. She was slender, with ash-blonde hair, calm gray eyes, and delicate, precisely carved features.

"Don't change your clothes," she said. "I want you to run to the store . . . oh, how was your day, dear?"

"The usual, except that—" But, no, she wasn't ready to mention her date.

"I walked home, and I'm hot and tired," she said in a complaining tone. "Can't Carrie go to the store?" She rode home on the bus. I saw her get on."

It was disturbing how the child in her sometimes erupted, like a bratty kid jumping out of a hiding place

16

and crying, "Boo!" The child in her wanted all her mother's attention, wanted to be first with her, just once. She wanted to be her oldest, her youngest, her only child.

"You could have ridden the bus, too, if you wanted to. Now don't give me an argument, Kate. You're too old to act like this." Her tone softened. "I need quite a few things, honey. It would be too much for Carrie to manage."

Poor little Carrie. At fourteen and a half she got out of everything because she was the baby of the family. As for Anne, even if she were home it would be no use to suggest her going to the store. "Anne went to the store when you were too little to go," she could hear her mother's voice.

Kate stood where she was, knowing how ugly she must look, her face set in stubborn, rebellious lines, her lower lip thrust out. And the funny part of it was she didn't mind going to the store. She just minded being the in-between daughter who was too young to be treated like an adult, too old to be treated like a child . . . who was never first with her parents but always in-between.

"Would you hurry, Kate? I need the carrots for the stew. The list is on the hall table."

"Sure, Mom."

The brat had gone back into hiding, and if she'd dared she would have run to her mother and given her a hug and kiss. *No use scaring her. She'd think I was sick.*

2

Kate felt a sense of family, and security, as she took her place at the dinner table. She knew kids who bragged that they never sat down for a family meal, except at the holidays. Sometimes she thought it would be fun just to snack—and there sure wouldn't be so many dishes to do. But most of the time, like now, she enjoyed sitting at the cloth-covered table, eating her mother's good home cooking, feeling the conversation flow around like a warm, familiar tide. This was the time the Flemings shared with each other the events of their day.

"Bill Sanders is going to retire at the end of the month," Mr. Fleming said. "I guess the crew will have to give him a send-off of some kind."

"We all know what kind of send-off you'll give him," Mrs. Fleming joked. "You'll all go to the House of Sirloin and get roaring drunk."

The girls laughed. They knew that Mel Fleming for one, would not get roaring drunk, unless a couple of beers would do it. He'd started as an installer for the telephone company and had worked up to supervisor.

He prided himself on a perfect record, never absent, never late. Kate looked at him with love, knowing how different her life could have been if he was not so steady, so hard-working. The dark hair, which she'd inherited from him, was now threaded with gray.

"School was hectic today," Anne, who was a freshman at Community College, offered. "I don't think I'll ever learn my way around that campus. By the time I found my Spanish class I was ten minutes late, and Mr. Alvarez gave me the dickens. At least I think he did. He spoke in Spanish, so I can't be sure."

As Kate joined in the ripple of laughter she was certain the instructor had not scolded Anne very severely. With ash-blonde hair, and gray-eyed like her mother, she had the same calm disposition, plus a special goodness that made everyone love her. Kate doubted that Anne had ever, in all her nineteen years, entertained a mean thought. She wouldn't be dating until Larry, her almost-fiancé, came back from college for the holidays, but she wouldn't mope, or doubt that Larry was living up to their agreement, too. She wouldn't once be tempted to cheat a little. Not Anne.

"How was your day, young one?" Mr. Fleming asked his youngest daughter.

Carrie happily took center stage. She had her father's dark hair and eyes, also his short stature. But where he carried himself with a bearing that deceived the eye into thinking he was at least average height, Carrie made a virtue of being short. She'd ask people to reach for things off shelves that she could have reached herself if she'd tried. She was as cute as a kitten whether her round, dimpled face was wreathed in smiles or set in a babyish pout.

"I recited in class today," she said, rolling her bright eyes to make full contact with each member of her audience. "I gave a book report on *Catcher in the Rye,* and I was *great.* Honest, I made everyone laugh, even Miss Harris."

"You're modest, too," Kate observed. She wanted it to sound like sisterly teasing, but it came out a bit harshly. There was a moment's silence, then Mr. Fleming addressed his middle daughter.

"And how was your day, Kate?"

If she wanted to she could startle them all with the news of her date with Ross Barrows. The Barrows family was prominent in Orange Grove, Mr. Barrows being the town's leading realtor, while Mrs. Barrows was active in community affairs. Her parents would know there must be something special about her that she'd attracted a boy from such a background. But she wasn't ready to make the announcement. She'd wait a day or two—just in case something went wrong.

"I spent most of my noon hour in the library, doing research for my essay on American heroes."

"That's nice," Mrs. Fleming murmured. Then said, "Carrie, wipe your chin—and push back your hair."

The girls divided the cleaning up, and after watching television for a while with their parents, went to their separate rooms. The single-level ranch house had a master suite plus three small bedrooms. Kate was grateful for the privacy of her own room as she posed in front of the mirrored closet door.

If only for one minute she could see herself as others saw her. Maybe she was more attractive than she realized, and could get by with acting kind of flirty with boys, but disdainful of them, too—drawing them on, yet holding them off, the way girls like Lela Granger did. Lela would look up at Ross, laughing and giving him deep glances from her lavender eyes, but if he

20

dropped an arm around her shoulders she'd more than likely frown and draw away. It was a game girls played when they were very sure of themselves.

How could Ross possibly have asked me for a date, Kate wondered, when he could go out with Lela? Maybe Lela had been too uppity with him, and he was punishing her. But what kind of punishment was that? Lela would laugh at him. "Is that the best you can do?" Kate could imagine her saying.

I'm the one who'll be punished. But, no, she wouldn't let that happen. She'd be happy with the one date —assuming he didn't change his mind about it. If she didn't expect any more than that she wouldn't be hurt.

She saw Ross in the hall the next day, but he didn't see her. He was with Lela who was almost as tall as he, slender and golden. She wore a T-shirt the pale lavender of her eyes, and a darker skirt that swung gracefully around her long legs. There was no right or wrong side of the tracks in Orange Grove, but there was an area toward the foothills where the houses were larger, and stood on half-acre plots that were professionally landscaped. The men were in business or the professions, the women belonged to garden and bridge clubs, did community work, or perhaps had careers of their own. Both Ross and Lela came from this background, and looked it. As they passed, Lela laughing and tossing her hank of golden hair, Ross smiling deeply into her eyes, Kate drew back against the wall, feeling plain and shabby in her discount-store blouse and skirt.

Kate was so thoughtful on the bus ride home that Doris asked what was eating her.

"I don't know whether to take Ross's invitation

seriously or not," Kate said quietly, although she knew she was dropping a bombshell.

"Ross who? What invitation?"

She'd decided she had to confide in someone, and Doris was her best friend.

"Ross Barrows. He asked me to go to the movies Friday night."

"You're kidding!"

"Thanks."

"I didn't mean it that way, Kate . . . yes, darn it, I did. Ross is a senior, and he's used to going out with girls like Lela Granger. Why would he suddenly ask you out?"

"Thanks again." But she couldn't be angry with Doris for voicing the thought that had been in her own mind ever since noon the day before. She drew a sigh. "You're right, Dee. Why would he? I thought at first maybe he and Lela had had a falling out, but I saw them together today and they were just about drowning in each other's eyes. Golly, she's beautiful." Another sigh. "I guess he just asked me out on impulse, and he's probably been kicking himself ever since."

"I don't know about that," Doris said. Now that she was over her surprise she was herself again. She loved to argue, and for that reason invariably disagreed with any position Kate took, an adolescent trait that could be pretty tiresome. But now Kate listened with interest as Doris played devil's advocate.

"Lela isn't all that beautiful. She just acts as if she is, and that creates an aura that makes people think she's beautiful. Besides, she has all those gorgeous clothes. Clothes aren't looks, though. You're every bit as good-looking as she is."

Kate gave her friend a wide-eyed stare. "Sometimes

22

you come out with the darnedest things, Dee. Even though you only said it for the sake of argument I think you're right about Lela. She isn't all that beautiful. Her face is too narrow, her neck is scrawny, and her eyes are sort of squinty. Still—"

"*Still,* my ankle. I don't know what's wrong with you, Kate. I should think you'd be tickled that Ross asked you out. Instead, you're making yourself miserable. Don't forget you have something Lela doesn't have."

"I do?"

Her friend wasn't arguing now, and Kate had an idea of what was coming. Doris envied her having sisters while she was an only child.

"You have a wonderful home life," Doris said, "with parents who really care about you—and two sisters. Lela's older sister ran off and got married when she was in her teens and she's never been home since. Lela's dad is in Public Relations. Most of his business is in L.A., and Lela's mother spends a lot of time up there, too. I guess you've heard of the parties Lela sometimes throws when they're away."

"No. I've never paid much attention to the gossip about kids like her."

Doris had the instincts of a gossip columnist, and eagerly filled Kate in on what she'd missed.

"They say that some of the kids skinny-dip. And they drink wine and beer. Once they got so noisy the neighbors called the police. When the Grangers found out they grounded Lela, but not for long. They just don't care that much. Just a couple of weeks ago she gave a party that went on most of the night."

"And I suppose Ross is at the top of her guest list."

"They live only a couple of doors apart, and his folks

23

are gone quite a bit, too. I guess that's the way it is with the upper crust. We're lucky we're lower-middle class."

Kate didn't like labels. And she didn't like what she'd just heard about Ross attending those wild parties. How could she deal with such a sophisticated boy? Her parents had asked all three girls to promise they wouldn't drink, at least until they were twenty-one. "You'll be of legal age then, so you won't be breaking the law. And you'll be old enough to make the decision as to whether you want to drink or not. You won't be yielding to peer pressure," Mrs. Fleming had said. The girls had all given their word.

Kate stared out the window until Doris spoke.

"Gee, I'd love to have a soda, but I'm broke."

Kate was anxious to get home now, to be alone in her room so she could think over all that had happened lately. But she couldn't let her friend down.

"I'll treat," she said.

When they got off the school bus they went to a snack shop in their neighborhood. Doris had a generous allowance, but she also had a sweet tooth and gobbled up most of her spending money within days of getting it.

"I feel awful about letting you treat, but thanks." Doris took a long pull on the straw that ended in a slurp, then went after the two big scoops of ice cream in the bottom of the tall glass.

"Don't mention it."

Kate sipped a Coke. She wasn't overweight, and her skin was good, but she wanted to keep it that way. Auburn-haired Doris was plump, and her fair skin broke out periodically. "Baby fat," she would say if Kate scolded her. "It'll go away soon. My skin will clear up, too, when my hormones get straightened out." She'd never had a date, but didn't seem to care. Maybe that was because she was an only child, and too close to her parents.

Am I really that lucky to have sisters, Kate wondered, even though I'm in the middle, and it seems as if no one would have missed me if I'd never come along?

"We'd better go," Doris said, after one last slurp. "Mama will be worrying about me."

They walked along the wide street, with the split-levels and ranch houses on both sides. All were well kept up, with neat lawns, shrubs and a few trees. When they came to Doris's gate she thanked Kate again for the treat. She started up the path, and then turned back.

"Don't worry about the date with Ross," she said. "You always worry about things, like when you have to recite in class. But then you always do okay."

Kate stared after the plump figure in the navy blue dress. Is Doris right? she wondered. Is that the way I am? I worry, but then I come through all right? She pondered the matter the rest of the way home. It would be so nice to be sure she had one trait that was all her own, that made her stand out. Anne didn't worry. She just went ahead, knowing she'd do well at whatever she undertook. Carrie didn't worry because she knew she'd get by on her cute ways, if nothing else.

She could imagine her mother talking to a neighbor. "You know how Kate is. She's a worrywart, but when it comes right down to it she always does fine."

Thursday Ross waved to Kate across the campus, his smile a reminder of their date. He was alone, leaning against a tree, an open book in his hand. As Kate waved back, her heart rocking, but her smile steady, she thought, Doris is right. I'm going to do okay. At least she was sure now that Ross would call for her Friday night. All the rest of the day she went around as if she were daydreaming. But she wasn't. It was real. It was true. She had a date with Ross Barrows.

That night at the dinner table, when her time came to give an account of her day she said, "Nothing special happened today, but tomorrow night I'm going to the movies with Ross Barrows."

Everyone spoke at once. Her father wanted to know if Ross was the son of the real estate man. Kate said he was.

Her mother said, "When Anne was sixteen she didn't *tell* us she was going on a date, she *asked* us. I don't know about this, Kate."

Anne spoke up, her gentle voice pouring oil on the water. "I know Ross. He was a year behind me in school, but he seemed to be an okay kid."

"Well, if you say so, Anne."

Kate knew she should be grateful to her older sister, and she was, but she felt angry, too, that Anne's word meant so much more in the family than hers did. She could have sworn to Ross's character, and it would have meant nothing.

Carrie's contribution didn't help her mood, either. "Ross wouldn't have asked you out if he knew what a slob you are. You left the bathroom in a mess this morning, Kate, and I'm calling a conference after dinner."

Years ago, when there'd been a squabble between the three girls about division of chores, their mother had suggested they have a conference and work out a solution - among themselves. The conference had worked so well it had become an institution. If one girl hogged the phone, borrowed another's clothes without permission, or committed any other offense that affected them all, a conference was called. It had worked fine throughout the years, but now it seemed childish to Kate.

"I'm sorry about the bathroom," she told her younger sister, "but I was late this morning. I was going to clean it up the minute I got home. Only—"

"Only I cleaned it up this morning. I *hate* a messy bathroom." Carrie, who only months ago had been a little pig, had now gone to the opposite extreme. "We're going to have a conference," she insisted. "That's the rule. Any of us has the right to call one."

"I'm afraid you'll have to count me out, honey," Anne said. "I have some homework I have to get to just the minute the dishes are done."

Carrie wasn't mollified by the gentle tone. "Now that you're in college you think you're too big and important for anything!"

Tears gathered in the round brown eyes, and Kate had a sense of how the younger girl felt. The conference was important to her, a part of her childhood, and she knew it was breaking up. She hadn't learned to accept the changes, the little wrenchings that were a part of growing up.

"We can have a conference by ourselves," Kate offered. "Anne can give you her proxy, so you'll have two votes."

"Just the two of us wouldn't be any fun." She pouted for a minute, then said grudgingly, "All right, we won't have a conference. Just promise you won't leave our bathroom in a mess anymore."

"I promise."

3

Kate had decided on a silky pearl-gray blouse, and a flannel skirt of darker gray, for her movie date. It was marvelous luck for her that gray was "in" this year, for it was her very best color. She'd been tempted to give herself one of the new soft perms, but had decided against it. It might make her look so different that Ross would notice, and guess what going out with him meant to her. Instead, she brushed her dark hair until it fell smooth and shiny, just below her ears. She put on very little makeup. It couldn't make her beautiful, anyway, so she might as well look like herself.

Promptly at seven-thirty the old black Mustang drove up. It wasn't just old, she knew, but a collector's item. She'd watched kids crowd around it at school, never dreaming she'd ever ride in it.

She would have run out when the car stopped out front, but she knew better. "When a boy calls for one of my girls he comes to the door," was her mother's rule. So she waited until the doorbell rang.

"Hi," she greeted Ross. "Won't you step in and meet my family?" That was another rule.

"Sure." He'd dressed nicely for the date in a beige corduroy jacket and brown slacks. His hair was still slightly damp from a shower. As she led him to the living room her heart felt ready to burst with pride.

Her mother sized him up in one comprehensive glance, and greeted him pleasantly. Her father took in his size and maturity, and paid him the compliment of standing up and shaking his hand. Anne had jumped up to lower the volume on the television.

"Hello, Ross. It's nice to see you again," she said.

He gave her the special smile everyone had for Anne. "Hi. How's Community College?"

Anne said it was fine, and then Carrie took the stage. Making eyes, and pouting at the same time, she asked Ross if he'd found a singer.

"Yes, we found one just today."

Carrie tossed her head. "I bet she can't sing any better than I can."

"She can't, but she's seventeen," Ross said with a big brother smile.

He laughed as they walked to the car. "You've got a nice family."

"Thanks."

She wasn't nervous until they were in the car and had decided on the movie they wanted to see. It was playing at a theater across town, and as Ross concentrated on driving, Kate felt it was up to her to put the conversational ball in motion. Only what did you talk about to a boy like Ross? They had no friends in common. Music was important to him, but she knew nothing about it, except what she liked, and she favored soft ballads over the rock that he was most likely in to. She looked out the window, searching for a topic of conversation, but nothing seemed worth commenting on. Her mouth got dry, and her palms got wet. Anything she said would sound stupid. She was so uptight now she wasn't even sure she could find her voice if she did think of something to say. It was just as she'd feared. She wasn't up to a date with a boy like Ross.

You always worry about things, like when you have to recite in class, but you always do okay, Doris had told her. Thanks, Dee, she thought.

"You have a brother, don't you?" she said. Again, thanks to Doris, she was in possession of this bit of information, this ice-breaker.

"Yes—good old Luke. He's up at Stanford."

"Oh," she said with respect. Stanford University, in the northern part of the state, had high scholastic standards.

"Yeah," Ross said, not missing her tone. "Luke's a brain." He was silent a moment, then he said, "I'm not up to Stanford. I guess I'll go to Community College for two years, then maybe finish at San Diego State."

She started to tell him that of course he was good enough for Stanford. Then she recalled how he'd frowned over the chemistry book. He was an honor student, but that didn't mean that learning came easy to him. Besides, his tone had been cheerful. It didn't seem to bother him that his brother excelled him in scholarship.

"There's nothing wrong with San Diego State," she said. "I may go there, too—if I decide to go to college."

He gave her a sideways glance from dark-blue eyes shadowed by stubby lashes. "Is there any doubt about it?"

"Yes. I'm just not sure what I want to do. Besides, it won't be easy for the folks to put us all through college. Anne has to go, of course, because she's a brain, like your brother. Carrie's smart, too."

"And you're not?"

"I don't know what I am," she said, then laughed and said, "I see you have a tape deck."

"Yes. I just had it put in. Would you like to hear some music?"

"I'd love to."

While he surprised her by turning on a country tape, she thought of how close she'd come to blurting out how she sometimes felt as if she didn't belong in the family. Anne and Carrie were both so special in their own way. Who needed a middle daughter? She was like a third bookend. But if she'd laid this on Ross he'd think it was sibling rivalry. And it wasn't. She didn't envy her sisters. She'd be satisfied to be herself—if only she knew who she was.

She was grateful for the music, afraid to talk any more now, for fear she'd say the wrong thing. Then they were in the parking lot, and there was the activity of getting out of the car, smoothing her skirt while he locked the door.

In the lobby he said, "Would you like some popcorn?"

She thought he spoke too politely, as if he was already bored with her, and instinctively she took on Carrie's protective coloring. Giggling, she said, "You wouldn't offer me popcorn if you'd ever heard me choke on it. I can disrupt a whole theater." She clutched her throat, and rolled her eyes, as if she were strangling—imitating Carrie at her clownish best.

He laughed, but rather hollowly, she thought. "How about a candy bar then?" His voice was quite restrained.

She'd made a mistake, and quickly set about correcting it. Raising her head with all the dignity of her older sister, she spoke in Anne's gentle tones. "Thank you. A candy bar would be nice."

31

She'd made the transition too quickly, and he gave her a rather startled look before buying a candy bar and a bag of popcorn.

When they were inside the darkened theater he asked where she'd like to sit. Not daring to use the personality of either of her sisters now, she was stuck for an answer. Should she state her preference for sitting halfway down, or leave it up to him?

"A—about halfway down, I guess . . . unless you'd prefer to sit closer—or farther back."

"Where do you usually sit?" People were looking at them, and he sounded impatient.

"Halfway down."

He took her arm, his hand big and forceful as he propelled her along the aisle. When they were seated she wondered whether to eat the candy bar right away, or to wait and see what he did. But he might be waiting for her. . . .

Tentatively, she began to unwrap the chocolate bar. He immediately dug into the popcorn. She'd made the right decision.

When she'd finished the bar she wiped her hands very carefully on a tissue, in case he should hold her hand. He didn't. He became engrossed in the picture, and after a while she was able to relax and enjoy it, too. When the lights went on he smiled at her, still half-lost in the film. They discussed it on the way to the car, agreeing that it had been funny, but serious, too.

"Where to now?" he said when he'd helped her into the car, and settled himself behind the wheel. "Would you like to go to The Pump and have a beer?"

I'd love to. She could hear herself speaking with cool assurance, as if going to The Pump was nothing new for her. But she didn't dare speak the words aloud. The tavern, just outside of town, was a favorite hangout for teenagers, but she knew she'd be out of her depths there. Besides, there was her promise to her parents that she wouldn't drink, at least until she was twenty-one.

Her hands were sweating again, and her throat was tight, as Ross looked at her, waiting for her answer. The parking lot lights were bright so that she could see the crease between his brows. How could she respond so that he wouldn't cross her off his list forever?

Anne would have told him quietly, "I don't drink." Carrie would have giggled and said, "Are you kidding? I'm high enough just being me. I don't have to guzzle beer."

Strange, she knew almost word for word what her sisters would say in any given situation, but she was never sure what she'd say until it was out.

"Maybe some other time," she heard herself say, "when I've cleared it with my folks to be out a bit later."

He nodded, not seeming displeased. "Let's go to Smokey's then and have a soda."

Smokey's was a teen hangout, too, although not many seniors went there. But if Ross felt out of place among the smaller, younger kids he gave no sign of it. Smiling good-naturedly, he pushed through the crowd until he found an empty booth. Kate barely acknowledged the greetings of kids she knew for fear they'd move in on them.

"How about a burger and Coke?" Ross asked.

She nodded eagerly, but remembered to eat carefully so as not to choke. The minute she was through eating, she vowed, she was going to be herself and make some intelligent conversation, just as if she was talking to Doris. She'd ask Ross about his music, whether he intended to make a career of it. She'd ask about the girl singer who'd just joined the trio. "Is she from Orange Grove High?" she'd inquire, an alert, interested expression on her face.

She pushed her plate aside, finally, and pulled the soda over in front of her. Ross did the same, looking at her expectantly, as if he somehow sensed that the evening was going to take a different turn.

"I've been meaning to ask you—" she began.

A high-pitched feminine voice cut her off.

"Ross! You're the last person in the world I'd expect to find at Smokey's. I'm entertaining my little cousin tonight, but what's your excuse for being here?"

Kate felt her heart sink like an anchor. She looked up in sick fascination at the golden girl who stood beside the booth . . . and she could have laughed bitterly when she remembered how she'd let Doris convince her that Lela Granger wasn't really beautiful. Oh, her face was narrow, all right—aristocratically so. Squinty eyes? Ha! Her lavender eyes were merely narrow, too, but long, with an upward tilt at the corners that gave her an exotic look. Scrawny neck? Not with the multiple gold chains she wore—real gold, as anyone could plainly see.

"Hi, Lela." Ross got to his feet rather slowly. Then smiling at the younger girl who stood beside Lela he said, "Hi, Midge."

The girl was probably twelve, a thin blonde child with a look of chronic discontent on her pinched face.

"Hello," she said in a whining voice. Then pulling at Lela's sleeve, "I wanta go. You promised I'd get home in time to see 'Monsters from the Void.'"

Lela pushed off the child's hand, and frowned as she looked at the smudge of chocolate on the sleeve of her white jersey dress. "See what you've done! Now be quiet a minute while I meet Ross's friend."

She erased the frown lines as if they were marks on a blackboard as she smiled at Ross. "Are you babysitting, too?"

"Hardly. Lela, this is Kate Fleming. She's a junior at Orange Grove. Kate, this is Lela Granger."

Narrow lavender eyes swept over Kate, taking in her nondescript looks, neither blonde nor brunette, taking in her personality, which was neither lively nor calm and dignified. The uptilted eyes put price tags on Kate's skirt and blouse, and the imitation gold necklace she wore. Blouse, $8.95. Skirt, $12.95. Chain, three dollars at the most.

"Kate Fleming," she repeated, rolling the name on her tongue. "Ross said you go to Orange Grove."

"Yes." A squeaky little voice like a mouse being quizzed by a cat.

"Funny, I've never noticed you . . . or maybe it isn't so funny. I take it you're not very prominent in school affairs."

Kate felt as if she were engulfed by flames, and yet she hadn't the presence of mind to even try to beat them out. She longed for Anne's composure, or Carrie's sense of the ridiculous. Either of her sisters could put this rude girl in her place. But she wasn't Anne or Carrie.

I'm somebody, though, and I won't be stepped on.

"No, I'm not very prominent in school affairs," she said, in a remarkably controlled voice. "I just mind my own business, get a B average, and try to avoid notoriety."

She'd scored a bull's-eye. The other girl knew she was referring to the wild parties she gave when her parents were away, that at least once had ended up with the police being called. The narrow face flamed, as Lela jerked Midge by the arm.

35

"Come on, if you want to see that stupid program." Then to Ross, in a heavy tone that was almost a threat. *"I'll see you later."* She gave Kate a parting look that was ninety percent venomous scorn, ten percent grudging respect, as if she'd met the enemy and learned that she was no pushover.

Ross laughed as he sat down. "What do you say we have another soda to take the taste out of our mouths? When Lela's in one of her moods she can make you think you've just drunk hemlock."

She hadn't expected Ross to discuss the other girl with her, and taken by surprise, she could think of nothing to say except that she'd enjoy another soda. As he continued to talk she was glad she hadn't responded to his remarks about Lela. It was plain that any problem between him and Lela was like a family squabble. Outsiders who intervened did so at their own risk.

"She's really a great girl," he said, "but she's been overindulged in some ways, neglected in others. We grew up only a few doors apart, you know, and sometimes old friends get the idea they own each other. She knew I was going out with you tonight and I guess she resented it, although we both date other people." He chuckled. "She must have guessed we'd come here after the show, and she borrowed Midge so she'd have an excuse to come here, too. I bet Midge got at least five bucks out of it."

Kate smiled, but said nothing. Once in a while she knew exactly how to behave without even thinking of how either of her sisters would act. This was one of the times.

"Well, I'd better get you home," Ross said. "Your first night out with me your folks are probably a little concerned. But one of these nights we'll go to The Pump, huh?"

Full of self-doubt again she hesitated, gulped, and said, "Sure."

He walked her to the door. The porch light was on, and they regarded each other rather gravely. She had a feeling the whole evening had led up to this moment. Would he kiss her good night? How should she respond? What did other girls do about kissing on a first date? She was sure Anne hadn't, but she would have handled it so beautifully the boy wouldn't have held it against her. Carrie hadn't been out on her first date yet, but when the time came she'd make a joke of it, if the boy wanted to kiss her, and he'd end up laughing.

Ross moved closer to her. As he inclined his head toward hers, she wondered if he could hear the wild thudding of her heart. She licked her lips so they wouldn't feel dry to him if he kissed her . . . *if she let him kiss her*. Then she thought that wet lips might be provocative, and she swiped her hand across her mouth.

"Well, I guess it's time to say good night." His voice was husky. "It was a nice evening." He brushed his cheek against her hair, then straightened up. Before she could speak he'd walked away.

"Thanks for the movie!" she called after him.

Lying in bed, so wide awake she felt as if she'd never sleep again, she went over the evening. She knew Ross better now, knew there was no arrogance in him, that he was good-natured, although she'd strained his patience a time or two with her indecision. He'd made it plain he expected to see her again.

There was just one thing that bothered her, and it

bothered her so badly it wiped out all her joy at how well everything else had gone. When he'd said that some night they'd go to The Pump she'd told him, "Sure."

What would she do when the time came—when she'd either have to go to the tavern with him, and drink some beer, or tell him flat out she didn't drink? "I promised my folks."

Would she have the courage to tell him that, or would she break her promise to her parents rather than risk losing him? *What kind of girl am I?* She wished she knew.

4

She thought that Ross might call her on Saturday, but he didn't. Saturday night she babysat for the Fletchers who lived on the next block. Some girls her age were working part-time in stores and fast-food restaurants, but she liked to babysit, and was reluctant to give it up. She felt it was the one thing she did well, and it made her feel useful. Parents needed to get out once in a while, and often there was no family member they could count on for babysitting. There'd be strain in a young mother's face when she went out in the evening, but she'd be calm and relaxed when she came home a few hours later, glad to get back to the babies that had got on her nerves a short time before.

Still, as she walked to the next block Kate reflected that she'd love to have some new clothes—a few really nice things now that she was dating Ross. She couldn't ask her folks to give her a larger clothing allowance than they did, and babysitting didn't pay enough to provide her with more than pocket money. It was a problem she'd have to face up to real soon.

Mr. Fletcher met her at the door. He smiled pleasantly as he said, "Come in. Mrs. Fletcher is putting on her face, or whatever you women do that takes so long when you go out."

It was thrilling the way he'd called her a woman, although it made her flush, too. She felt like an imposter, knowing there was still a little girl inside her, a little girl who was even bratty at times. Then the two little boys came running, shrieking her name. They'd cried the first few times she'd stayed with them, but now they were tickled when she came to sit.

"Hi, Jamie. Hello, Teddy." She knelt down and hugged five-year-old Jamie, then swung Teddy, who was three, up into her arms. A minute later, Mrs. Fletcher came from the back of the house. She was nicely dressed and made up, and smelled of a flowery perfume.

"We'll be home no later than midnight," she told Kate.

Kate nodded. Some people were very unfair with sitters, not coming home when they said they would. After a few bad experiences Kate had learned to have a clear understanding with anyone she sat for. If they didn't return at the agreed on time, barring an emergency—in which case they were to call her—she wouldn't sit for them again. And if she sat longer than agreed upon she expected to be paid extra.

"All right, what do you guys want to do?" she asked when she was alone with the two youngsters.

"Watch TV!" Jamie answered promptly.

"TV!" Teddy echoed, clapping his plump little hands.

"Wouldn't it be more fun if I read to you? We'll read some more about Mowgli and his friends."

Reading had always been one of her greatest pleasures, and it would be nice if she could pass on the habit

40

to some of the children she sat with. Many parents didn't have time to read to their kids—or didn't take the time. The two little boys would remember the Mowgli stories long after they'd forget a television comedy.

"All right, you can read to us," Jamie finally said, and Teddy nodded solemnly in agreement. She gave him an impulsive hug before going to the bookshelf, and taking down the Jungle Books which she'd started reading to the boys the last time she'd sat with them.

She read aloud until Teddy began to nod, then she carried him to bed, loving the feel of his warm little body, relaxed so confidently against her. After slipping him into bed she pulled the covers up to his dimpled chin. When she kissed his forehead it was softer than her velour top.

"Good night, little fellow. Sleep tight."

She read to Jamie for half an hour more, then put him to bed. She was pleased when he asked if she'd read more about Mowgli and Shere Khan, and Akela next time. Maybe I should be a teacher, she thought. But she wasn't sure. Some girls her age knew what they wanted to do with their lives. Not her. There were so many possibilities, and she didn't feel that she knew herself well enough to plan ahead.

She wandered through the quiet house, indulging in her favorite daydream when she sat. The house was hers. The sleeping children were hers. There was a man sitting in an easy chair in front of the fireplace, and he was hers, too. He'd always been a shadowy figure, but now he'd taken on definite dimensions and coloring. He was tall and wide-shouldered with rust-colored hair and dark-blue eyes.

"Are the kids asleep?" he asked her in his deep voice.

"Yes, they're dead to the world. And no wonder, the way they ran their legs off all day long."

"And you ran after them. You're tired, aren't you, dear? Come sit here, and rest your head in my lap." He patted the ottoman beside his chair.

It was a lovely dream, but she shook it off after a time. The thought returned that she was getting too old to babysit. She wasn't earning enough money, and she wasn't getting any experience in the job market. Anne had started buying her own clothes when she was sixteen, working part-time in a dress shop. Much of what she'd learned would be useful to her when she went into merchandising, which was her ambition.

But Anne was a natural saleslady, in a quiet, helpful way. She was clever at sewing, too, so could do alterations. Kate came back to the fact that the one thing she was good at was babysitting. If only there was some way she could make more money at it, turn it into a sort of business.

She got some chips and a Coke from the refrigerator which she had the Fletcher's permission to do, and went to the family room. The big TV set was tempting, but she didn't turn it on. An idea was beginning to form in her mind. Babysitting as a business—why not? Good sitters were hard to come by, yet many girls complained they couldn't get sitting jobs. Some people were afraid to trust young girls they knew nothing about, and some girls made it worse by irresponsible behavior, raiding the refrigerator of everything that was in it, talking on the phone all night, even having their friends in without permission.

What if she organized some girls? She could train them, get jobs for them, and charge a commission. It would be a business, like an employment agency.

Her mind went into high gear. How would she get

the jobs? She could advertise in the neighborhood shopping news, put notices on the bulletin boards in supermarkets.

How would she recruit the girls? She laughed, thinking maybe she could start with Carrie and Doris. Doris was sixteen, but she was immature and didn't know how to go about getting babysitting jobs. She'd be glad to sit, though, if she got the chance. *She's immature, and I'm not?* Passing thought. Maybe she could get permission to put a notice on the bulletin board at school, asking girls who were interested in babysitting jobs to get in touch with her.

As she munched potato chips, and washed them down with Coke, her mind raced on. She'd draw up a set of rules for her sitters . . . no raiding the refrigerator beyond whatever snacks they had permission to eat. No phone calls, unless there was some emergency. No entertaining friends without permission.

There'd also be rules for the parents. They must tell the girl where they could be reached, return home when they said they would, pay the agreed-upon sum at the end of the evening. Kate had had trouble with one or two people she'd worked for on that score. A girl couldn't afford to go back time and again for her money.

Oh, and they'd have to see that the girl got safely home. And they mustn't leave a sick child. She'd been scared half to death once when a baby who supposedly only had a slight cold suddenly ran a high temperature.

The list went on, and by the time the Fletchers returned Kate had done most of the "think" work, and it only remained to start putting her plan into action.

"Thank you, Kate," Mrs. Fletcher said as she paid her. "We can count on you next Saturday night, can't we?"

Kate shook her head. "I'm sorry, but I won't be sitting anymore."

Mrs. Fletcher smiled ruefully. "I knew it was too good to last. You've started steady dating, haven't you?"

"I'm dating some, but it isn't that. I'm going on seventeen and I need to earn more money."

Mr. Fletcher spoke up. "We could pay you a little more."

"No," Kate said hastily. "I don't want that. I plan to start a babysitting agency. I hope you'll hire one of my girls. I'll guarantee the reliability of any girl I send you."

The couple exchanged glances. Mr. Fletcher gave a slight nod, and his wife said, "If you recommend a girl we'll give her a try."

She had her first customer! Walking home, with Mr. Fletcher watching her from the sidewalk until she was inside her gate, she tried to grasp what had happened that night. She'd got an idea, worked out the details, and had already started to put her plan into effect. She'd soon be a businesswoman, in a small way. It was pretty amazing for a girl who'd always thought she was as useless as a third bookend.

Sunday was family day. Over a late breakfast the weekly outing was planned. Orange Grove was within twenty miles of the ocean, to the west, not much farther from the desert to the east, and in between there were wooded mountains where they sometimes picnicked. Disneyland was a short drive to the north, and San Diego's Sea World an even shorter ride away. Then there was the Wild Animal Park, practically in their backyard.

Carrie wanted to go to Disneyland. Anne quietly

44

suggested the coast. Kate said she didn't care where they went. The thought uppermost in her mind was that some time during the day she was going to tell her family about her business venture. Would they laugh at her? Or for once would her parents see her as an important member of the family? She could see her mother's gray eyes fixed on her as if she were seeing her in a new light. She could hear her dad saying that he was proud of her. "Girls, what do you think of your sister?"

What her dad was actually saying was, "With the price of gas what it is I think we'd better stay pretty close to home. How about the Wild Animal Park today?"

"That's fine with me." For once Kate was the first to speak. She felt a new confidence in herself now that she'd soon be a businesswoman.

"I always enjoy the Wild Animal Park," Anne said, as she got up and started to clear the table.

"We never get to go to Disneyland!" Carrie complained.

"We were there only a month ago," Mrs. Fleming said. "Now get up and help with the dishes so we can get started."

They rode on the Wagasa Bushline Monorail, and observed the animals from all parts of the world roaming in an environment that was as close to its natural habitat as could be managed. Kate studied the wild creatures with mixed feelings. She was fascinated, as always, at the sight of grazing gnus, of giraffs loping across an open plain, and herds of elephants refreshing themselves at a water hole. Yet she was aware that the lions drowsing in the California sun were not free, in spite of the large area that had been set aside for them.

45

Did they realize they were captives? As they slept, did they dream of a distant land where there were no barriers in any direction, where they were the lords of creation?

"You're quiet, Kate," her father said.

How often one of her parents made that comment. Usually she had no answer that would make sense to them, and she had none now. If she mentioned her concern for the animals her dad would cite facts and figures that would prove they were better off than they'd be on the plains of Africa, or in the jungles of Asia.

"I was just thinking," she said vaguely. And it was answer enough as the ride ended and they went into the thatched-roof refreshment building.

When they'd loaded their trays Kate offered to pay.

"Why should you?" Carrie asked. "Do you know why you're always offering to treat? You're trying to make people like you." Carrie had recently been exposed to psychology and it had infected her like a germ.

"I'm not always offering to treat!" Yet Kate recalled how she'd bought Doris a soda only two days before. Was she really trying to buy people, or was she generous by nature? This was no time to try to solve the mystery of Kate Fleming. They'd reached the cashier. "Please, Dad, I want to pay! I'll explain in a minute."

"Well, all right," her father said.

When they were seated she told of her plans. "I'm going to start a babysitting service. That's why I wanted to treat. I'll soon be a businesswoman."

"I think it's a dumb idea," Carrie offered. "Why should girls pay you part of what they earn?"

"Because I'll get the jobs for them, and see that they're treated fairly."

Anne, as always, was encouraging. "That's a clever idea, Kate. I wouldn't have thought of it in a hundred years. I bet you're going to make a great success of it."

"Sounds like our Kate has a head for business," Mr. Fleming observed, looking at his wife.

The opinion that mattered most to Kate was slow in coming. Her mother looked at her with thoughtful gray eyes and finally said, "I guess it's worth a try." Her attention was immediately diverted to her youngest daughter. "Carrie, you're making an awful mess of that chili dog." She took a paper napkin, dipped it in her glass of water, and wiped some catsup from Carrie's chin.

"Mama, I'm not a baby!"

"Then you shouldn't act like one."

As the familiar exchange went on Kate grappled with her disappointment that her idea of starting a business was of less importance to her mother than wiping a dab of catsup off Carrie's chin.

She felt deflated for only a moment. Her idea was still a great one, and tomorrow she'd start putting it into effect. Tomorrow she'd also see Ross. He might even see her, she thought with a slightly rueful smile.

5

She'd convinced herself she was now special to Ross, not as special as Lela, but surely he'd have his eye out for her. Ever since Friday night she'd been storing up things to tell him in case they got to talking. She'd been tongue-tied a good part of Friday night, but now she thought she could be more relaxed with him. Her business enterprise gave her a new confidence in herself. The minute she got to school Monday morning she'd gone to her counselor and asked if she could put a notice on the bulletin board announcing that she needed girls for her babysitting service. Mrs. Morris had told her she'd have to consult "the powers that be," but her smile was encouraging.

"That's very enterprising of you, Kate. I'll let you know tomorrow."

Now she prowled the halls, and just before the bell rang for first period she saw Ross. He was with two other boys she didn't know. One was tall and thin and wore steel-rimmed glasses. The other was shorter and solidly built. Ross walked between them, looking from one boy to the other. He definitely was not glancing around, hoping to catch sight of Kate Fleming.

She went to the library at noon. If he wanted to find her he'd look for her there. She took a book from the shelf and sat at the same table she'd sat at when he'd first noticed her. She watched the door for sight of a tall, wide-shouldered figure, a rust-colored head, and a pair of dark-blue eyes. It would be funny if the library became "their place," because she already knew he wasn't very studious.

When the bell rang she regretted having spent the entire noon hour in the library. He was probably outside, enjoying the fall sunshine.

Between afternoon classes she prowled the halls again . . . and just before last period she saw him with Lela. They were holding hands as they walked along —just as if Lela hadn't acted like a witch Friday night and he hadn't confided to Kate that the golden-haired girl sometimes left a taste in his mouth as if he'd drunk hemlock.

Tuesday Kate got permission to put up a sign on the school bulletin board. "Kate's Babysitting Service needs sitters. Call—" And she added her phone number.

That evening she got two calls. She arranged to interview the two girls at noon the next day, just outside the cafeteria.

She was talking to one of the girls, a shy fifteen-year-old, when she saw Ross. He was heading for the cafeteria, and he was alone. If she'd moved just a foot or two she would have been in his path, where he couldn't help seeing her. He'd probably ask her to have lunch with him . . . but the girl was anxiously querying her about a job, and she had no choice but to give her her full attention.

"I need to earn some money to help out at home," Marylou said, "but most of the people in my neighborhood are older, and don't need sitters. And mom's afraid to let me answer ads in the paper."

"Give me your full name, address and telephone number." Kate opened a notebook she'd bought for just this purpose. When she'd taken down the information the girl gave her she said, "I'll try to have something for you very soon. And your parents don't have to worry. I'll visit every home and see that it's okay before I send any of my girls out."

By the time Marylou had walked off, and Kate had entered the cafeteria Ross was sitting with the two boys she'd seen him with before. Kate decided to have her sandwich and milk outside.

After school Doris wanted to stop for a soda, but Kate told her she had some business to attend to.

"I've started a babysitting service. I have to have some cards printed, and get an ad in the Shopper."

Doris's mouth turned down. "I don't see why you have to start a business. Why can't you just go on sitting?"

"Because I'm growing up, and there's not enough money in it, and not enough challenge."

"Everything will be different now," Doris complained. "You won't have any time for your friends."

"Sure I will."

But Doris sulked until the bus was halfway to their neighborhood. Then she suddenly brightened. "Maybe you can get a job for me. I've never known how to go about it."

"You bet. Just give me a little time."

When they got off the bus Doris went home, but Kate walked to the shopping center. First she went to the Kopy Kat, a place that did copying and quick, inexpensive printing. She ordered five hundred cards that said Kate's Dependable Babysitting Service. Her address and phone number would be in the lower corners. Next she went to the Oak Tree Shopper where she placed a small ad that was to be run until further notice. She was quite proud of the ad she'd composed.

"You supply the baby, we'll supply the sitter. Trained, responsible teenagers."

Her next stop was the supermarket where the manager, who knew her well from all the grocery shopping she'd done for her mother, smilingly gave his permission for her to tack a notice on the bulletin board, offering the services of "qualified babysitters."

When she arrived home, tired, flushed, but triumphant, her mother's customary greeting caught her by surprise.

"Don't change your clothes, Kate. I want you to run to the store for me."

She didn't think it was the brat inside her who flared up. It just wasn't fair that she had to run all the errands.

"I've been all over the shopping center, getting my business started. I'm tired and hungry. Why do I have to go to the store when Carrie's sitting in the family room watching some dumb program on TV?"

Her mother spoke in the soft, too patient tone that she often used with her middle daughter.

"I'm glad you have this little enterprise to occupy you, Kate, but you mustn't think that you can neglect your regular chores because of it. The list is on the hall table."

Now she did feel the brat taking over. "Why can't Carrie go to the store for once? Why does it always have to be me?"

"You know very well that Carrie does her chores. But you're older, and—"

51

"If I'm so old why can't I have my own phone in my room, like Anne?"

"You're not that old."

"I get it. I'm old enough to run all the errands around here, but not old enough to have any privileges."

Her mother's patience was beginning to fray around the edges. "I declare, I don't know what gets in to you at times, Kate. What kind of girl are you that you make such a fuss over running a little errand for your mother?"

I don't know, Mom. I don't know what kind of girl I am. I know I'm not angelic like your dear Anne, or cute like your little Carrie. But I am somebody. If you prick me I'll bleed, so please don't stab me with your eyes like that.

"If it will make you feel any better," her mother said more gently, as if she'd read her thoughts, "Carrie is watching a program on public television that's part of her homework."

"Okay, Mom. Can I have something to eat before I go?"

"Of course, Kate. My goodness!"

That evening Kate set up a bookkeeping system. She entered the names and telephone numbers of the two girls who had applied for sitting jobs on file cards. Next she outlined a list of rules for both sitters and parents, writing in the scrawl that only she could read. Later she'd type the material, and run off copies.

It was a good thing she had her interest in the babysitting service, she thought over the next few days, otherwise she didn't know how she could have stood the disappointment of Ross ignoring her just as if they'd never had a date. She saw him every place, it

52

seemed, in the halls, the cafeteria, across campus—
sometimes alone, sometimes with a crowd, more often
with the two boys who seemed to be his special friends.
Or he'd be with Lela.

Kate tried not to blame him for not seeing her, even
though he sometimes passed within a few feet of her.
His rust-colored head stood out like a beacon, inches
above that of most other people, while she was so
ordinary—average height, dark hair—that there was
nothing about her to draw his eyes.

Sometimes even the joy she felt in how well her
business was going deserted her, and she wallowed in
misery, wishing he'd never asked her out at all. There
was not only her private hurt that it had ended with one
date, there was the embarrassment of telling Doris
every day, "No, I haven't talked to him."

"You mean *he* hasn't talked to *you*," Doris said one
day.

It was true, but Kate was so angry at the cruel
remark that she walked home on Friday rather than to
ride the bus with Doris. And to think I got her her first
babysitting job, she brooded as she walked along.
Saturday night Doris was going to sit for the Fletchers.

She was halfway home when Jeff drove up beside
her.

"Want a lift?"

"No, thank you."

"Want to go to the coast tomorrow? Some of us are
going over and fool around a while."

She knew who the kids would be, boys and girls from
the neighborhood, none of them over sixteen. She
knew what the fooling around would amount to.
They'd play in the sand like youngsters, wander
through the shops, laughing at everything they saw, eat
so much junk somebody would probably get sick on the

ride home. She used to have fun that way, too, but now it sounded awful to her.

"You want to come?" Jeff urged.

Suddenly she was afraid to turn him down. Maybe she'd never have another date with Ross. She'd sit at home every night, unless she went some place with Doris.

"I'm not sure," she said. "Call me tonight."

"Why should I call you tonight when I'm talking to you now? We're going to leave early tomorrow morning, and if you don't want to come I'm going to ask someone else."

He spoke so heatedly that his voice broke, as if it was still changing. Probably it was, and now her mind was made up.

"Thanks, Jeff, but—"

"But no thanks, huh?"

"I have other plans," she said, which was only half a lie as she planned to stay home in case Ross should call.

Jeff glowered at her from under corn-colored hair that half-covered his green, white-lashed eyes.

"Maybe I'll have other plans after this!"

They'd quarreled like this when they were ten, and she was suddenly bored with it. Yet she had a gentle feeling toward him she'd never had before.

"Thanks for asking me," she said.

"Don't mention it." The sarcasm was so heavy his voice broke again.

She looked sadly after him as he roared off in a cloud of exhaust fumes. *Good-bye, Jeff.*

The weekend would have been unendurable if she hadn't been kept busy with her babysitting business.

She received numerous calls, both from girls wanting jobs and parents looking for sitters. She explained the rules to both, promised to provide both jobs and sitters.

Sunday the family went to Sea World, in San Diego. Then at last Monday came.

Monday they nearly ran in to each other in the hall. Kate was hurrying to world history and had opened her book to check the date of the Boxer Rebellion, when she suddenly sensed a large, solid object bearing down on her from the opposite direction. She and the large, solid object skidded to a stop just in time to avoid a collision.

"I'm sorry!" she gasped.

"My fault," Ross said. His dark-blue eyes looked at her anxiously. "Are you all right? You must have thought I was going to run you down."

"I'm fine. I was cramming, too." He had an open book in his hand . . . advanced algebra this time.

"Where have you been keeping yourself?" he said. "I haven't seen you around."

She could have laughed and said, "You haven't looked very hard." But of course she didn't. It was too good to be talking to him, to be standing so close to him, to entertain any negative thoughts.

Borrowing Anne's composure she said, "I've been pretty busy, too. You know how it is."

"Yeah." He closed the book and shuffled his feet.

"Well, I'll see you," she said, flashing Carrie's grin. She wasn't going to wait for him to walk off and leave her standing there. As she turned away he caught her arm.

"The trio is going to practice after school," he said.

"We have permission to use the music room. Would you like to stick around? I'll drive you home later."

"I'd love to!"

"Okay. See you in the music room right after last period."

"You bet."

Only later did she worry that she'd been too eager. She couldn't imagine Anne practically jumping for joy because a boy had asked her to sit by while he practiced with his musician friends. First she would have reflected a moment, making sure she hadn't promised to come right home after school. Then, if she found she was free, she would have smiled pleasantly and said, "Why, yes, I'd like to." Not, "I'd love to!" and "You bet," without a moment's hesitation. Carrie would have been enthusiastic, of course, but she was always enthusiastic, so it wouldn't have sounded as if it was the most exciting thing that had ever happened to her.

Yet Ross had grinned before loping off down the hall, as if he was pleased with her response.

The afternoon would never end. She was convinced of that before it was half over. The hands on the big clock at the front of the room seemed frozen . . . but then at last the bell rang, and then another bell, and finally the school day was over.

She didn't exactly run to the music room, but she certainly didn't dawdle, either. When she reached the room, at the far end of the building, Ross was already there. So was the tall boy who wore steel-rimmed glasses, and the shorter, heavy-set boy she'd seen Ross with a number of times. There was a girl there, too, a girl she knew to be a senior, although she knew nothing else about her.

"Hi, Kate, come and meet the gang." Ross held out his hand, and when she went forward he clasped it lightly around her arm as he made the introductions. "Kate, this is Tamara. No last name as far as the group is concerned. Just Tamara, and some day it's going to be a household word. She's our singer," he added.

Tamara's smile made light of the words, but she had a look of quiet determination about her that made Kate think she would become a famous singer if that was her ambition. She had short, curly brown hair, and brown eyes that burned with intensity. Her sturdy body seemed packed with energy. She wasn't beautiful but Kate thought that under a spotlight, with a mike in her hand, she'd look very showbiz.

"I'm glad you came to rehearsal, Kate," she said in a low-pitched, vibrant voice. "Even an audience of one makes it exciting."

"I'm glad to be here." Kate felt a little shy with the other girl, as if she were already a celebrity, but she had the feeling they were going to become friends.

The tall boy, Oren, had the same intense look about him Tamara had. There was an electric guitar over his shoulder, and he greeted Kate absent-mindedly as he started to tune the instrument.

Stan, the heavy-set boy went to the piano after greeting Kate with a friendly grin. Ross, on drums, completed the trio.

Kate sat on a hard-backed chair and for more than an hour listened as the group went from country music to rock, followed by a medley of standards. It was clear Oren was the leader of the small combo, as well as the arranger.

"Let's take that over from the top," he'd order. Sometimes he'd change a passage. "I don't like that phrasing." He'd strum by himself for a while. "There, that's the way it should be."

Stan played well, and Tamara sang with a fervor that made the roots of Kate's hair tingle. Yet Kate's eyes were all for Ross. He seemed to enjoy playing drums, but without getting carried away by the music as the others did. He was the one who finally said, "Let's call it quits for today."

"That's okay with me," Stan said. "Let's go out to The Pump and unwind."

Oren nodded his agreement. Tamara, brushing curly brown hair back from her flushed cheeks said, "My throat is parched. That beer is going to taste awfully good."

Ross turned to Kate with a smile. "You're coming, too."

Her heart took a plunge as if she were on an elevator that had suddenly dropped twenty floors. She hadn't expected the subject of The Pump to come up so soon. She'd hoped that by the time it did she and Ross would be closer, so close that she could tell him about her promise to her folks.

When she didn't answer he said a bit impatiently, "Well, how about it, Kate? The kids want to get going."

She died inside. Ross was a musician, and he needed the release of a beer or two with his group after a practice session. Why had her parents exacted such a promise? How had Anne lived up to it?

"I—" Even as her lips moved she didn't know what she was going to say. I'll pretend I'm Carrie and say something funny. Everyone will laugh and forget what an oddball I am, a sixteen-year-old girl who doesn't dare take a sip of beer.

Ross spoke again, ignoring her tentative "I."

"We can stay out there and have a bite of supper. They make great corned beef sandwiches."

Without being aware of it he'd thrown her a lifeline. "I'm afraid my parents are hopelessly old-fashioned, in some ways," she said. "We all have to be at the family dinner table, promptly at six-thirty, unless we've given prior notice that we're staying out." She didn't mind admitting that much. It was reasonable for a mother to insist on knowing how many people she was preparing dinner for.

Ross's smile that had wavered for a moment now returned. "You guys go ahead," he said. "Kate and I will join you next time."

"Okay," Stan said, "but it would be more fun if we all went."

"Shut up, Stan," Tamara said. "You heard the girl. Her parents expect her home for dinner."

Kate couldn't bear to think she was causing dissention in the group. "You go, too, Ross," she urged. "I can get home alone. It's only three miles, and I love to walk."

His face was unsmiling, but he didn't seem annoyed as he said, "I wouldn't think of it. I said I'd drive you home and I will. We can guzzle beer with these guys some other time."

A reprieve! She hadn't lost him—not yet.

They carefully locked the music room where Ross had left his drums, and trooped to the parking lot behind the school. Tamara, Oren and Stan piled into an old station wagon, Stan taking the wheel. On the side of the vehicle was a painted sign that said The Music Makers.

When the station wagon had roared off with shouted "Good-bye's!" Ross smiled at Kate. "So you like to walk, do you?"

She nodded, wondering what he was getting at.

"Then how about walking out to the grove?" he said. "You can stay out a while longer, can't you?"

"Oh, yes! I don't even have to call unless I'm going to be late for dinner."

"Then let's go!"

6

They crossed the parking lot and started across the field that separated the school grounds from an old orange grove. Once oranges had been a valuable crop in the area, but now, with the building boom, only a few neglected trees remained.

The ground was springy under Kate's feet, and in a sudden burst of high spirits she broke into a run.

"Oh, you want to race, do you?" Ross said, catching her mood.

"Yes, and I'll beat you, too! Last one to the grove is a rotten egg."

She didn't stop to think of what a childish taunt it was. The late afternoon sun overhead, the soft earth beneath her feet, seemed to lift her out of herself. She could fly if she wanted to!

He loped along beside her for a few yards, then with a laugh sprinted ahead. "Slowpoke!" he threw over his shoulder.

Her breath was coming hard and she had a pain in her side by the time she reached the grove where he was waiting for her, a big grin on his face.

"So you finally made it," he teased.

"It wasn't a fair race. You're a track star," she panted.

"I'm going out for track, but I'm not likely to be a star," he said. "Anyway, no alibis are accepted. You lost, and you have to pay the price."

"What price? Do I have to roll a peanut down Orange Avenue with my nose?"

"No. You're really going to learn the agony of defeat. You have to do this."

He caught her by the shoulders, brought her forward until their bodies were lightly touching, and pressed a kiss on her lips. She was so taken by surprise she had no chance to do anything, to move her head away, even to press her lips tightly together. Her mouth was soft and receptive as if she wanted to kiss him. Did she? Before she could decide he'd let her go, and was once more· grinning at her.

"There, that should teach you not to challenge people."

Laughter bubbled up in her throat. "I've learned my lesson, sir."

"Okay, just so that's understood." He picked two oranges and spread his jacket on the ground. "Be seated, fair lady."

They sat close together—the jacket didn't permit them to sit otherwise—and they ate the oranges which they agreed were the sweetest they'd ever tasted.

"It's probably because they're grown naturally, without fertilizer or a lot of water," Ross speculated.

"I love natural things."

"I guess I do, too, although I've never really thought about it. You do a lot of thinking, don't you, Kate?"

"Oh, I don't know." Did he think she was some kind of nut who brooded about things? *Maybe I am.* It killed her when someone carelessly started a forest fire, or bulldozed an area of virgin soil.

But Ross didn't pursue the subject. Looking up at the clear blue sky through the branches of the orange tree he said, "This is even better than going out to The Pump. It's okay to unwind with a few beers, but this is relaxing, too, and it won't leave us with an H.O."

"H.O.?"

He looked at her as if he wasn't sure he'd heard the question right. "Hangover," he said. "Don't tell me you've never had a hangover."

This was a good opportunity to start preparing him for the truth. "No, I really haven't," she said.

"Smart girl. I'm pretty careful, myself, not to drink too much. But once or twice I've got carried away, so I know how miserable a hangover can be."

"Do you plan to make a career of music?" she asked, anxious to change the subject.

"No, I'm not that good," he said. "It's just a hobby with me. Oren will make it as a pro. So will Tamara. Stan I'm not sure about." He pulled up his knees and wrapped his arms around them. "So far I haven't found anything that I'm really good at, or so interested in I'd want to make a career of it. I'd like to try a lot of things, have all kinds of experiences before I settle down to any one thing. I may end up doing some oddball thing like running a bait shop over on the coast, or scratching out a living with a few cabins and a gas pump out in the desert." He smiled. "Or I may end up selling real estate like my dad."

"I don't know what I want to do, either," Kate said. "I like kids, but I don't think I want to be a teacher. It's the little preschoolers I'm crazy about. I've done quite a bit of babysitting, and now I've started a business."

She was so full of her idea that she told him all about it, and only became self-conscious when she'd finished.

"Goodness, I don't know why I rattled on like that. I must have bored you to death."

"I'm only bored by people who are bored themselves," he said. "I think you have a great idea, Kate. I should think it could even lead to a full-time career."

She'd thought the same thing. With more women working out all the time why shouldn't there be a career in caring for preschool children? It would take some special training, though—probably some kind of degree.

Ross looked at her closely as if trying to decide if she was serious about her idea, or if it was just a temporary enthusiasm. And all of a sudden she became doubtful. Was she the kind of girl who stuck with things, like Anne, who'd known what she wanted to do since she was fifteen? Or was she a scatterbrain like Carrie? Of course Carrie would get by, being cute and appealing.

In her uncertainty about herself she lowered her head, and her nervous fingers plucked out a blade of grass. She studied it as if it held the world, like Blake's grain of sand. The blade of grass was coarse and brown, although in the spring it had no doubt been tender and green. Next spring it would turn green again . . . or it might die during the winter.

Ross rose abruptly. "I'd better get you home," he said. "I don't want you to be late for that family dinner."

Was he mocking her? No, she decided. But he was probably bored. The only people who bored him, he'd told her, were people who were bored themselves, and perhaps that was the impression she'd given with her contemplation of the blade of grass. And she couldn't explain. How silly he'd think her if she told him it had set her to thinking of life, and death and re-birth.

"Don't you have to get home, too?" she asked.

"My folks are going out to dinner, some doings at the country club."

As they walked back across the field she wanted to invite him to dinner at her house, but she was afraid he wouldn't want to come, and she'd force him to turn her down, embarrassing them both . . . or he might feel obliged to accept and spend a miserable evening.

They didn't talk much as he drove her home. She glanced at his profile occasionally. It was a very handsome profile, the forehead gently curved, the nose straight, the jaw strong. She wished he'd turn to her for a moment so she could look into the dark-blue eyes that softened his face, but he stared straight ahead as if the light traffic demanded his full attention. He probably regretted not going to The Pump with the others. He'd have a couple of beers under his belt now, be laughing and talking with kids who spoke his language.

Yet she recalled how he'd looked up at the blue sky and said, "This is even a better way to unwind than drinking beer." He'd seemed happy to be with her. He'd shared a good deal of himself with her, telling her how he hadn't decided what to do with his life. And he'd listened with interest when she'd told him about her babysitting business.

He stopped the Mustang in front of her house and faced her. His smile was pleasant, but when he met her eyes his glance didn't go below the surface.

"Good-bye," he said.

"Good-bye. And thanks for letting me sit in on the practice session. I really enjoyed it."

He gave a little shrug as if it were nothing. He didn't

say, You'll have to do it again some time. He'd no doubt concluded that she didn't fit in with his group.

"I'll see you," he said.

She jumped out of the car and ran for the front door. It was so easy to say, "I'll see you." But was she in for another agonizing wait before they got together again? It wouldn't even have happened that day if they hadn't literally run in to each other.

He'd kissed her, though. It had been impulsive, and over in a single heartbeat, but still it must have meant something to him. . . . She'd managed to stall him again on going to The Pump. As she'd thought earlier that day, if he got so he really liked her she could tell him about her promise to her folks. Surely he'd respect her for honoring a promise.

He might respect her, but would he want to go out with her? And what was there about her to make him like her so much that he didn't mind her not being able to share in his social life?

She opened the door, forcing all thoughts of Ross and The Pump from her mind. "I'm home, Mom!" It was almost dinnertime.

"All right, dear!" her mother called from the kitchen. "Get washed up. We'll sit down in five minutes."

Tuesday she saw Ross in the cafeteria. He smiled and waved, but he didn't cross the room to join her. Her sandwich turned dry in her mouth. The more she'd thought of the way he'd talked to her the day before the more she'd convinced herself that she meant something special to him. She wanted to be his girl, to have people say their names in one breath. Ross and Kate. But a girl is so helpless.

"All we can do is wait," she mumbled.

"What?" Doris asked, taking the chair beside her.

"Nothing. I was just thinking aloud."

"Well, don't. It's annoying, and you do it all the time."

"I do not! I hardly ever do it. What's the matter with you, anyway? I've never seen you so grumpy."

"Nothing's the matter with me. Just leave me alone."

"If you want me to leave you alone why did you sit down here? There are plenty of other places."

"All right, I'll find another place."

Kate stared after her friend as she flounced away and took a seat with some sophomore girls she didn't even know.

Puzzled, disturbed, Kate got up and started for the door. Halfway across the room she saw Ross and Lela at a table together. Neither one of them saw her. She might as well not have existed.

Doris acting like an angry stranger, Ross drowning in Lela's lavender eyes again—life was a mess. Or maybe *she* was. But then her spirits got a boost as a younger girl stopped her at the door.

"You're Kate, aren't you—who has the babysitting agency?"

"Why, yes. Are you interested in sitting?"

"Yes. Mom won't let me go out on my own, but if you investigate the home and everything—"

"I do." Kate reached in her bag and brought out one of her printed cards. "Call me this evening and I'll tell you all about it."

She'd had more calls for the coming weekend from people who wanted sitters than she had girls to send out, so another sitter was more than welcome.

Kate automatically sat beside Doris on the school bus. Even though Doris was still sulking for some reason it would have seemed odd to sit beside anyone else.

They rode in silence for a while, then Kate could stand it no longer. "If I've done anything to make you mad I'm sorry. So lighten up, will you, Dee?"

Doris turned to her and, shockingly, her eyes were brimming with tears. "I'm the one who should apologize," she half-sobbed.

"It's all right, let's forget it." She thought Doris was apologizing for her bad behavior that noon, and to show her she held no grudge she said, "Let's have a soda, huh? If you're broke I'll treat." *And not because I'm trying to buy your friendship, Dr. Carrie Freud notwithstanding.*

Doris shook her head. "Thanks, Kate, but I couldn't get down a soda."

Kate stared at her friend. "You're sick! That's why you've been acting so funny."

"I'm not sick." Doris faced her, chin up, in an almost defiant gesture. Her eyes were dry now.

"Jeff asked me to go to a party with him this Friday night, and I said I would. If you want to be mad at me go ahead, but you're dating Ross now."

Surprise. Confusion. A quick stab of jealousy. Only she didn't know who she was jealous of, Jeff or Doris.

"Who says I'm going out with Ross? I've had only one real date with him, and I may never go out with him again!" She was surprised at how angry she sounded.

"You *will* go out with him again—you'll have lots of dates with him. I've seen the way he looks at you."

At the moment that didn't matter. Doris and Jeff. *And she always pretended she wasn't interested in boys.* She looked more closely and saw that Doris had changed lately. She was still a bit plump, but she must have lost a few pounds. There were still a few blotches on her skin, but it had cleared up some and the lovely peach tone that so often went with auburn hair was emerging.

They had been close, closer than sisters in many ways, but Kate remembered how freely Doris had let her go when she'd become interested in Ross. *Come on, Kate, give her your blessing, even if it hurts. You'll get over it.*

"It's all right, Dee," she said. "I hope you have a great time at the party."

"Gee, thanks, Kate. We're still friends then?"

"You bet."

7

She gave up hoping for Ross to look her up at school, or to call her at home. He could easily have got her phone number if he wanted to call. There were only a few Flemings in the book. She saw him everywhere, in the halls, the cafeteria, on campus, but he seldom saw her, and if he did he'd merely smile and give a friendly wave.

How do you figure boys? She was sure he'd enjoyed their movie date, at least moderately. And she couldn't forget how happy he'd seemed the day they went to the orange grove, how comfortable he had appeared to be with her as he talked about his future, which he was so doubtful about. He seemed to realize she'd understand how he could toy with the idea of doing some odd-ball thing like running a bait shop on the coast, or some tourist cabins and a gas pump in the desert—or end up in real estate like his dad.

Did he talk that way to Lela? She saw them together often, but Lela always seemed to be doing the talking. Kate couldn't imagine her listening intently while Ross shared his inner thoughts with her.

Yet she only saw them in public. How did she know what went on between them when they were alone? They'd grown up together. They were probably much closer than he and Kate could ever be.

Thank goodness, she had her business to divert her thoughts. People told other people about her service. Girls constantly sought her out in school. She even got calls from girls in other schools, who had friends at Orange Grove High. Once in a while a girl gave her a bad time.

"I don't see why you should get part of what I earn," a sophomore named Faye said belligerently one day. "If I do the sitting I should get all the money."

"Then find your own jobs, and don't tell me when the people stay out later than they say they will and don't offer extra pay, or if the kids are unmanageable."

She was very sure of herself where her business was concerned. Still, it hurt her that Faye started a rumor that she was taking advantage of the girls who worked for her. It ended with her counselor calling her in.

"I got permission for you to put your notice on the bulletin board and I want to be sure you're being fair with the girls who sign up with you," Mrs. Morris said.

Burning with indignation Kate offered facts and figures, how hard she worked, her "overhead," which she'd learned was the term used for business expenses.

"I ride all over town, on the buses, or my bike, visiting every home before I send a girl there. If there isn't a respectable-looking woman in the family I turn down the job. I spend hours every week keeping up on my records. I have the cost of advertising and printing. I'll soon have to get an answering machine because my mother is getting tired of taking the calls that come in during the day."

Mrs. Morris held up both hands as if to ward off the pelting of words. "All right, Kate, I'm convinced. I think you're doing a fine job, and offering a real service to the community."

"Thanks, Mrs. Morris."

But Kate was still steaming as she left the office. Was life always like this? Did someone always try to spoil things? Was part of growing up learning to cope with unjust criticism?

"I've been looking everywhere for you, Kate Fleming."

Every thought she'd ever had fled her mind. Ross had looked everywhere for her. He was smiling more broadly at her than he ever had before, his eyes crinkled at the corners and a dent in his left cheek that would have been a dimple if his face weren't so lean.

"You've—been looking for me?"

"I sure have. We're playing a gig Friday night—nothing exciting, just a teen dance at the Community Center. We won't get to dance much, just at intermission, when they play records. But if you'd like to come—"

"I'd love to!"

"I have to get there early to set up my drums, so if you could get there by yourself—"

"Sure . . . no problem at all."

"That's great. You're really an understanding girl, Kate."

She'd been in a delirium of joy, but now her mind was clearing fast. What did he mean "understanding?" Did he mean that most girls wouldn't be willing to get to the Community Center on their own, or that they wouldn't be willing to sit by while he played drums? She knew he meant it as a compliment, but wasn't it really a put-down? She knew instinctively that Anne would not have accepted such a proposition. She would have been very gracious and sweet, would have found some way to decline that would not have been rude. But she would have declined.

Carrie would have exploded, "I should hike to the Community Center and sit around like a dummy while you play with your group? Forget it!"

Yes, almost word for word that was what Carrie would say. But she wasn't Carrie, or Anne. She couldn't bear to turn down his invitation. Still, she didn't want him to think she was lacking in pride.

In Anne's gentle tones she told him, "I try to be understanding. That's the least we can do in this world, isn't it?"

He was no longer smiling. "Yeah, I guess," he mumbled.

She hadn't sounded like Anne at all. The tone, even the words were right, but they didn't sound right coming from her. Worried, miserable, she looked up at him wishing she could explain that she didn't mind the arrangement Friday night, she just didn't want him to think she had no pride. She did. It was just a different kind of pride than her sisters, and probably most other girls had. She didn't mind putting herself out for a boy she cared for.

Before she could say anything the bell rang. "Oops, we'd better get to class," Ross said, as if the bell was a reprieve. Then—"I'll see you Friday night."

The minute he'd turned away she felt a rush of self-confidence. If she didn't mind the arrangement why should she act grudging about it? "You bet!" she called after him.

He looked over his shoulder, surprised but pleased.

He gave a little salute before loping off down the hall.

Kate was worried about what her folks would say when she announced she was going to the Community Center alone, but that Ross would drive her home. When the family sat down for dinner Friday night she still hadn't mentioned it.

And then there was no opportunity. Carrie was sulking and storming by turns because she'd been forbidden to double-date with a girl friend and two neighborhood boys.

"Eat your dinner, Carrie," Mrs. Fleming said quietly.

"I won't! I'm on a hunger strike!"

"Now, Carrie," her father said. "You know we're only thinking of what's best for you. Fourteen is too young to date."

"I'm fourteen and a half. And all Sharon and I are going to do is walk to the movies with Doug and Allan."

"There'd be more to it than that, and you know it," Mrs. Fleming said. "You'll sit together in the theater, and probably want to go some place for snacks afterward. That's dating, young lady, no matter what you want to call it."

"You'll never let me date! You'll always treat me like a baby!"

Mrs. Fleming reached over and patted her cheek. "You're too pretty to frown like that, honey. You're very precious to us. That's why we're strict with you. Let's have a smile now, and we'll see if we can't think of some treat for you. Maybe Daddy and I will take you to the drive-in movie."

Carrie had always loved to go to the outdoor theater,

but her smile was slow in coming. The folks *were* treating her like a baby, Kate thought. She was pretty sure there'd have been no objections if she'd wanted to walk to the movies with Jeff when she was fourteen and a half. *You're very precious to us. That's why we're strict with you.*

"All right," Carrie said at last, "but I want to go to the drive-in in Junction City."

"You drive a hard bargain, young one," Mr. Fleming said with a smile. "But all right, we'll have a backyard picnic next Sunday to make up for the extra gas we'll use driving to Junction City."

Carrie gobbled a few bites of food, then went to the telephone to tell Sharon she couldn't go to the movies with her and the boys. In the meantime Anne jumped up and started to clear the table.

"I'll do the dishes tonight," she volunteered, "since you're all going out."

"That's awfully sweet of you, dear," Mrs. Fleming said, giving her oldest daughter a loving smile. Then she turned to Kate. "What are your plans for the evening? Anne says you're going out."

Kate gave the same story she'd previously given Anne. "There's a dance at the Community Center. I thought I'd drop in."

"Are you going with Doris?"

"No, Doris is going with Jeff. I'll—sort of be Ross's date. He's going to drive me home."

She'd had to tell the whole story, after all, and a frown puckered her mother's usually serene brow. "Why doesn't Ross pick you up?"

"He's playing for the dance and he has to get set up, and sort of help out."

"I don't know about this, Kate." Her mother looked closely at her, and was about to say something else when Carrie appeared in the doorway, a jacket over her arm.

"If we're going, let's go," she said in her most imperious tone.

Mrs. Fleming touched a napkin to her lips and stood up. "Just don't be too late," she told Kate.

How late is too late, Mom? Or aren't there any rules for me?

"You run along and get dressed," Anne said when the door had closed behind the parents and their youngest daughter.

"I'll help you, Anne. There's no reason you should do all these dishes alone."

"And there's no reason I shouldn't. I have nothing else to do."

How could anyone be as good as Anne? She was kind, generous, thoughtful, but never with a hint of martyrdom. Her goodness seemed to flow straight from the core of her being. No wonder her parents had a special place for her in their hearts. No wonder Larry loved her. There'd been a slightly wistful note in her voice, though, as she'd said, "I have nothing else to do."

"You miss Larry awfully, don't you?" Kate said.

Anne nodded her ash-blonde head. "Awfully. I was wishing he could get home for a visit before the holidays, but he says he can't. Between his part-time job and the heavy courses he's taking he just can't make it." A smile brightened her clear gray eyes. "I just may get up to San Francisco for a weekend, though. I could stay with Joan."

Joan was an Orange Grove girl who was also going to San Francisco State.

"Oh, Anne, that would be super!" Kate cried. "When are you going?"

Anne laughed. "Impatient Kate. If you get an idea one minute you go with it the next, like your babysitting business . . . I'll have to wait a while on this. There are quite a few things to consider. It has to be the best time for Larry. And I have to save a little more money."

"I'll lend you some!"

Anne gave her most loving smile, at the same time she shook her head. "That's generous of you, honey, but I'll manage. Go along now, and make yourself pretty for Ross."

While Kate dressed she thought of what Anne had said about her being impatient. And she hadn't said it as if it was a fault—more as if it was the kind of impatience that led to accomplishment. She'd said she was generous, too. Did she really possess these two qualities? And if so how many more did she possess? What were they?

I don't possess self-confidence. If she did she'd wear the pretty new dress she'd bought in hopes Ross would ask her for a date. It was a gauzy print with a snug bodice and a graceful skirt—the most flattering thing she'd ever owned. But Ross might think she was silly getting all dressed up for what wasn't really a date. She put on a fringed denim skirt, a blue-checkered shirt, and deciding she might as well go Western all the way, she tied a white scarf at her throat.

"Hi, cowgirl," Ross greeted her when the first set ended and he joined her at the table near the bandstand she'd staked out.

"Hi." She greeted him shyly. He looked like a real professional musician in a glittering outfit that matched what the other members of the group wore, rhinestones on denim jumpsuits.

"Did you have any trouble getting here?" he asked.

"No. The bus dropped me off right in front."

The others joined them now, crowding chairs in around the small table. The boys went for soft drinks. Tamara pushed back her hair. She was flushed, her eyes bright from the excitement of performing. The glittering jumpsuit made her, too, look so professional that Kate was momentarily in awe of her.

"Whew!" she said. "It was hot up there under the lights."

"A Coke will cool you off . . . you sang beautifully," Kate said.

"Thanks, Kate. It was nice to have you sitting here applauding."

The boys came back with the Cokes. After taking a long swig of his Ross stood up, and pulled Kate to her feet. "We'd better dance while we can."

It was pure bliss to be in his arms while a record played a smooth, danceable number. He didn't hold her too close, just close enough so she could feel the lean hardness of his body as he guided her around the crowded floor. Her face came to the hollow of his shoulder, and it was all she could do not to snuggle against it.

"I'm glad you could come," he said, his voice a bit husky as his cheek brushed her hair.

"I'm glad you asked me."

He drew her close for a moment, in what seemed like a rush of affection. He really likes me, she thought. I must stop doubting him.

When they got back to the table the others had finished their soft drinks and were standing up.

"We're going backstage," Oren said. "I want to go over what we're going to do this next set."

"I'll be with you in a minute," Ross said.

They sat down and Ross finished his Coke. "I'm

sorry I can't spend more time with you," he said, "but
Oren is a slave-driver." He put his hand on hers, gave
her the warm smile that made her feel good all over.
"We'll go somewhere when this is over."

Where? she wondered, but tried not to think of it.
Her heart expanded with pride when Ross came onto
the stage a few minutes later, along with the others. She
hardly took her eyes off him the rest of the set. There
were a few kids present she knew, but none she was
really friends with, so no one came to the table. She
halfway thought—feared—that Lela might show up as
she had when she and Ross had gone to the movies, but
she didn't. Perhaps the Center was too common for
her, since many of the kids who attended affairs there
simply couldn't afford to go any place else.

She danced with Ross once more, during the second
intermission. Then at last the final number had been
played, and the hall began to clear. Tamara joined her
at the table while the boys loaded the drums and guitar
into the station wagon. When they came back Stan
spoke.

"Come on, girls, we're going out to The Pump."

"That's the best idea you've had all evening,"
Tamara said. "It almost makes up for some of those
clinkers you hit that nearly threw me off-key."

She was grinning, excited by the large audience she'd
had. Stan ran his hand through her mop of brown curls
to show he took no offense.

"You mean I hit a couple of sour notes, old lady?"

"I'm Oren's old lady, so keep your hands to yourself."

Kate had suspected that Tamara and Oren were in
love, but this was the first time it had been confirmed.
She hardly registered the fact, though, for her nervous-
ness. The time had come when she had to make a

decision—an impossible decision, either way. She'd either have to go to The Pump and drink some beer, or tell Ross she didn't drink.

"Let's go," Oren said. "That was a good work-out tonight. We've all earned a few beers—even Kate for stimulating the applause."

Ross pulled her by the arm. "Come on, cowgirl. You heard what the man said."

She smiled weakly. "Yes, but—but I'm afraid I can't go with you. I—Saturday is the busiest day for my babysitting business. The phone will start ringing before eight, and—" She hadn't known what she was going to say until she'd started talking. "And I just have to get home," she finished miserably.

Ross was smiling, but there was a groove between his brows she'd never seen before. "Being up an hour or two later won't make that much difference."

"I'm afraid it will. If I don't wake up and take the calls myself my folks will—will make me give up the business."

He'd been pulling her by the arm. Now he let her go so abruptly that she fell back a step or two before righting herself.

"If you really want to go home I'll take you home, of course," he said coolly.

They were all staring at her with varying degrees of disapproval. Tamara's eyes were shrewd as if she knew there was something wrong here, that no girl would put a little extra sleep ahead of being with Ross. Oren studied her through his steel-rimmed glasses, probing deeply, perhaps deciding that she was a disturbing factor in the group.

Stan, usually so good-natured, said roughly, "Take her home, Ross, and come out later. She's too young to go to The Pump, anyway."

This was terrible, the worst thing that could have happened. If Ross became convinced she was too young to go to a tavern with him he might decide she was too young to go out with. In desperation she lashed out at Stan.

"If you don't want me to go around with the group just say so, but don't say I'm too young."

"Hey, I didn't mean it like that," Stan said.

"Then why did you say it?" Ross demanded angrily of the other boy.

Oren's carefully controlled voice was a reproach to Kate as he said, "All right, cool it, you fellows. I don't want any fighting in the group." He turned a stern face on Ross. "We'll go out to The Pump. Join us if you want to."

"Try to make it," Tamara said to Ross. "It's more fun when we're all together."

And I thought we were going to be friends. But it wasn't Tamara's fault. The group did belong together.

When she and Ross were in the car Kate said, "Please just drop me at home and go out to The Pump. I feel awful, keeping you away from your friends."

He gave a little shrug, but didn't answer. The silence became unbearable as they drove along the nearly deserted streets. At last he ran a hand through his hair, and she knew it was a preliminary to his speaking.

"I guess I should admire you for taking your business so seriously," he said. His voice was gruff, but then it softened. "And, really, I do admire you, Kate. Not many girls would put business before pleasure."

Desperate to put things completely right between them she said in Carrie's bubbly voice, "I'll get to The Pump yet. I know I'd have a terrific time. I like to unwind, too, you know." Still Carrie, she reached over and tickled his chin.

He laughed, and batted away her hand. "It isn't safe to tickle the driver."

She didn't think he was amused, in spite of his laughter. And again he fell silent, until they reached her house. "I see the lights are on," he said then. "I guess you want to go right inside."

"Yes." What else could she say? "Thanks, Ross."

"What for? It wasn't much of an evening for you."

She couldn't bear for him to feel that way. "It was," she insisted. "I loved hearing you play."

"You mean it?"

"Yes."

"I'm glad, Kate. Sometimes I'm not sure how you feel." He gave her a quick kiss, said, "Good night," and the next minute she was flying up the path, so happy she wanted to wake the whole neighborhood to tell them her good news. Ross wasn't angry with her. The evening had ended with a kiss.

Her mother was alone in the living room. It looked very much as if she'd waited up for her, which was a surprise.

"Hi, Mom. How was the movie?"

"Fine. How was your evening?"

"Okay."

Her mother's smile was rather arch. "Only okay?"

"Well—"

"Why don't you come in and sit down, Kate? I've been thinking we should have a little talk."

Embarrassment. Dismay. My gosh, she told me about pollination when I was twelve, Kate thought. But maybe this is an advanced course. She moved shyly into the room and took the place her mother patted, on the sofa beside her.

"Is there anything you want to talk about, Kate?"

How could she be so embarrassed with her own mother? But she was, and found herself taking refuge in Carrie's impish personality. "I thought you were the one who wanted to talk."

Her mother looked at her with puzzled eyes, then smiled. "I did suggest it," she said, "but I thought you might want to talk, and be too shy to mention it."

"Me shy?" She laughed loudly.

"Well, no, you're not exactly shy. But—you're not exactly bold either." She looked down at her hands that were folded in her lap, and twisted her wedding ring around and around. When she looked up again there was the strained look on her face that Kate thought of as her "Kate" look.

"Since you're going with Ross, an older boy, and a boy from a slightly different background than yours I thought you might have some special problem you wanted to talk over. But if you don't that's fine. You've always been more independent than your sisters."

"Have I?" Kate asked eagerly.

"Why, yes." She evidently hadn't meant it as a compliment, and she seemed surprised and put off by Kate's response. "You'd better get to bed," she said crossly. "If you start getting calls early in the morning you'd better answer the phone promptly or you'll hear from the rest of us."

"Yes, Mom, I'll catch it on the first ring." But she didn't get up from the sofa. Now that she and her mother were talking she wanted it to go on and on. Sometimes Anne and her mother talked for hours in quiet voices, woman to woman. "Mom—"

"Yes?"

"Nothing, I guess."

"If you have something to say, Kate, for goodness sake, say it."

How much do I matter to you, Mom? I'm not your big girl, and I'm not your baby. What am I? I need to know.

"I just wanted to say that—that I'll be sure to catch the phone the minute it rings."

A sigh. "All right, dear. Good night."

8

Monday, for the first time, Ross came up to her in the cafeteria. She'd brought a sandwich from home, had picked up soup and milk and taken her usual place where she expected Doris to join her. In fact, she didn't even look up when a tray was placed on the table beside hers.

"Mind if I join you?"

"Ross! No, I don't mind at all." She wondered if she looked as flushed as she felt, if her words were too eager, her smile too bright.

"You sure you weren't expecting anyone else?"

"No, I wasn't. Doris and I usually have lunch together, but she didn't show today. Oh, there she is now, with Jeff." Doris and Jeff, lost to the world as they tried to find a table together. Doris with only a cottage cheese salad on her tray, Jeff with his corn-colored hair slicked back.

Ross took a few bites of meat loaf and mashed potatoes. Then he wiped his mouth and said, "I've been meaning to ask you if you're going with anyone else."

Was he asking her to go steady? Her heart seemed to leap up into her throat and she had to draw a deep breath before she could trust herself to speak.

"I've dated a little bit," she said at last, "but I'm not going with anyone right now."

He smiled. "Yes, you are. You're going with me."

She couldn't eat another bite. If she'd tried she would have choked. She couldn't speak, either. She could only smile at him and hope he'd guess how happy she was to be his girl. She kept waiting for him to say that from now on he wouldn't be going with anyone else, but he only smiled back at her, and after a minute he went on eating his meat loaf and mashed potatoes. He even ate the peas and carrots, and a piece of carrot cake which he washed down with a glass of milk.

"You didn't eat your lunch," he said when he was through. He looked from her plate to her, and she was about to murmur that she wasn't hungry when Lela's high-pitched voice spoke from across the table.

"Hi, you two. Mind if Hank and I sit with you?"

"Help yourselves," Ross said. "We're almost through. I was just coaxing Kate to eat a little bit more."

"What kind of girl has to be coaxed to eat? I'm always starved," Lela said. "Oh, Hank, you know Ross, of course, but do you know this girl? A—Kate." Eyes that were more blue than lavender today, reflecting the larkspur-blue of her body-hugging jersey top looked mockingly at Kate, telling her she was so unimportant she could barely remember her name, although she'd just heard it.

"Glad to meet you, Kate." Hank said.

She knew him by sight. He'd made Orange Grove's football team a contender for the high school championship in their conference almost single-handedly, and was a school hero. She'd cheered him from the bleachers more than once, thinking that any boy who played so savagely must be something of a brute, but she saw now she'd been wrong. He was as friendly and ingratiating as a big shaggy dog.

"It's nice to meet you, Hank." Her voice was warm and friendly, and if she hadn't been careful it would have been a bit pitying. It was as clear as could be to her that Lela was using the big, good-natured football player for her own purposes. And her purpose was to make Ross jealous.

Ross spoke pleasantly to the other boy. "Sit down, Hank, and take a couple of hundred pounds off your feet." He didn't speak to Lela. Was he trying to show her that her scheme wasn't working? But if he was really not jealous would he feel the need to show her, wouldn't he just be friendly but casual?

"What did you do Friday night?" Lela asked Ross when she was seated. "I thought you might show up at Mickey's party."

Kate didn't know if Mickey was a girl or boy, and she wasn't supposed to know. That was Lela's strategy, to carry on a conversation with Ross that would exclude her.

"The group played at the Community Center," Ross said. "I thought you might show up there." His smile was rather taunting.

Lela tossed back her head and laughed. "Really! Only the worst kind of losers attend affairs at the Community Center."

"They looked like pretty nice kids to me," Ross said. "Nobody had to be thrown out. That's more than you can say for some of Mickey's parties."

Kate looked from one to the other with the feeling

she was watching a tennis match. No, it was more like a duel. Lela acknowledged Ross's thrust with a tight smile, then thrust back.

"At least his parties are never dull. He invites only the prettiest girls and the most exciting guys."

"I guess that's why he didn't bother to invite me."

"Not at all. You qualify, and you know it. But with Hank and I going together he may have been afraid you wouldn't bring the right type of girl."

Kate caught her breath as if she'd been sprayed with cold water. But either Ross didn't know the barb was for her, or he didn't care.

"Ready to go, Kate?" he asked in a matter-of-fact tone, as he pushed back his chair.

She nodded mutely, and stood up. Ross took her by the elbow and led her toward the door. As she reviewed the exchange between him and Lela she recalled that she'd pitied Hank for being used by Lela. Was she being used by Ross for the same reason—to make the person he really cared for jealous?

When they were in the hall he turned Kate so that she was facing him, his hands light on her shoulders. He was still holding her as he said, "I'd have shut her up if I'd thought you wanted me to. But I had a hunch you didn't. You're smart enough to know she was just trying to get a rise out of us."

Was she that smart? Or was she dumb to try to hold Ross when a girl like Lela wanted him? Did he know his own feelings, even? She was convinced now he wouldn't deliberately use her to make Lela jealous. Perhaps he was tired of Lela's shrill voice, her nasty moods, her possessiveness, and wanted to go with a quiet, agreeable girl for a change. But he and Lela went back a long way, and Lela had formidable weapons with which to win him back . . . her aristocratic beauty, her wardrobe of flattering clothes, the many friends they had in common.

She remembered what her mother had said about her being independent. That meant she didn't let anyone push her around, or to put her in a position where she'd be stepped on.

"I didn't care for Lela's remarks," she said, moving away from Ross's hands, "but I'm glad you didn't make an issue of it. I want to make it plain, though, that I wouldn't expect to put up with much of that."

She studied his face, and saw his eyes widen in surprise. He'd evidently thought she was a meek little mouse. He might not like her as a girl who was too independent to put up with the rudeness of his old friends.

But after a moment he nodded. "I wouldn't expect you to. Hey, we've got a few minutes. Want to take a walk?"

"Sure."

They strolled around the campus. She saw girls eyeing her enviously. Boys looked at her, too, in a more interested way than they had before . . . perhaps they were wondering what Ross saw in her.

She wondered, too. Her burst of self-confidence had burned itself out. So she had a streak of independence. She wouldn't be walked on even if she had to go it alone. That didn't make her an exciting person, the kind of girl an attractive boy like Ross was likely to fall in love with.

As she looked at him their glances met. "I like your eyes," he said, probing deeply. "Gray, aren't they? With your dark hair they really stand out. They're the first thing I noticed about you."

She'd sometimes wondered if the contrast between

her hair and eyes was attractive or freakish, but she'd never wonder again.

"I got my eyes from my mother, my hair from my dad," she said, smiling up at him, flushed with pleasure. Telling her he liked her eyes was the first compliment he'd paid her.

He took her hand and swung it as they walked. They didn't talk for a minute or two, but it was all right. There was no awkwardness in the silence. Then he spoke.

"I really enjoyed having you in the audience Friday night. You're sure you weren't bored?"

"No, I wasn't bored at all. Did—did the others resent it that you took me home instead of going to The Pump with them?"

"I don't care if they did or not. We make music together. Outside of that what I do is my own business. But to answer your question, no. They understood that you had to get home. Oh, we're going to have a practice session at my house after school tomorrow. We can't get the music room here at school, so Mom said she'll put in earplugs just this once. Want to be an audience of one?"

She smiled and nodded, hiding her dismay. She'd meet his mother after school tomorrow. She felt herself shrink at the thought, become small and drab as an English sparrow. Every mother must have a mental picture of the girl her son would fall in love with. And when she had an exceptionally handsome, popular son she would surely picture him with a girl who was pretty and popular, a girl who was superior in every way. She could hear Mrs. Barrows asking Ross, "What in the world do you see in that girl?"

"Don't forget tomorrow afternoon," Ross said as the bell rang and they hurried toward the building.

"I won't," she said, wondering that he didn't hear the rueful laughter in her voice.

She tried not to worry about going to Ross's house. She did her homework when she got home from school, took some phone calls from people wanting sitters, lined up girls to fill the jobs, then went to the family room. Carrie was sitting cross-legged on the floor, two feet away from the television. Anne and her mother were in the room, Anne with a schoolbook in her lap, Mrs. Fleming working the needlepoint that was her hobby.

As Kate passed the chair where her mother sat she was struck by how lovely the needlepoint piece was that she was working on. Stopping to admire it she said, "I bet you could sell your work, Mom, if you wanted to. There's a gift shop over in the mall where they take handmade things on consignment. Mrs. LaCross, who runs it, hires sitters from me. That's how I happen to know about the things being on consignment. That means—"

"I know what it means, Kate, but the very idea of me selling my needlepoint is silly. It's just a hobby. It isn't good enough for anyone to buy it."

"It's beautiful," Kate insisted. She studied the basket of violets her mother had almost finished. "If you'll let me, Mom, I'll talk to Mrs. LaCross. You've made more chair covers and wall hangings than you know what to do with. Why not sell some of them and make a little money?" She laughed, excited by her idea. "You'll be running a cottage industry."

Her mother shook her head. "It's not enough that you've gone into business, now you want to turn me into a businesswoman. You'll have Carrie running a business next."

Mrs. Fleming was joking, but Kate answered seriously. "I'm thinking of putting her to work as a sitter. Mrs. Fletcher says she'll give her a chance."

Carrie jumped up, wildly excited. "Can I, Mom? Can I?" She'd been wanting to sit for some time but her mother had insisted she was too young.

"We'll see," Mrs. Fleming said.

"No!" Carrie shrieked. "I want you to say I can— right now."

Kate put in quietly, but as urgently as she knew how, "The Fletchers will see she gets home safely, and I'll give her extra coaching on what to do and what not to do."

"Well, all right. She can try it, I guess."

Carrie ran and gave her mother a hug, grinned her thanks at Kate, then went back to her cross-legged position in front of the television.

Kate was pleased, but not satisfied yet. "I'm going to speak to Mrs. LaCross, Mom—all right?"

Her mother looked as doubtful as if she was being asked to head up a giant corporation. Kate tried to imagine what a big step it was for her. She'd married at nineteen, going from her parents' home to her husband's. She'd worked seven days a week all those years, becoming expert in a dozen different fields, cooking, cleaning, nursing, bookkeeping, but because she'd never been paid for her efforts in cash she couldn't believe she was capable of earning money.

"You can speak to Mrs. LaCross," she said at last, "but that doesn't mean I'm going to go through with it."

Oh, yes, it does, Kate thought, knowing she'd won. She wished she could hug her mother as Carrie had, but for some reason she couldn't. Plopping on the sofa, beside Anne, she asked her what she was studying.

"English lit," Anne answered in her usual quiet voice . . . no, her voice was even quieter than usual. Her gray eyes were unfocused as she looked up from the book. Kate had the feeling her sister didn't see her at all, that her mind was far away. Perhaps in San Francisco? She'd mentioned a short time ago that she planned to go there and visit Larry.

Why didn't she go? She'd said she was short of money, but surely she could swing it if she wanted to go this badly. She was actually pale, and there were shadows under her eyes.

"English lit. Umm," Kate said. She wished she could find some way to comfort her sister, but she'd already offered to lend her the money to take the trip, and been turned down.

Anne abruptly stood up. "I'll start dinner, Mother," she said.

"That's a good girl. I'll be in in a minute to help you."

Anne walked listlessly to the kitchen. Mrs. Fleming did a bit more work on the basket of violets, then put away her needlepoint and followed Anne to the kitchen. Kate tried to concentrate on the quiz show Carrie found so exciting, but it was no use. All she could think of was tomorrow afternoon, going to Ross's house, meeting his mother. Should she dress up? No, that would be silly. They'd be going right from school. Anyway, it wasn't the way she dressed that was so important. Mrs. Barrows was more likely to judge her by the way she acted. If only she had more poise, more self-confidence—if she only dared to be herself.

But what am I?

Her thoughts broke off as she heard a most unusual sound coming from the kitchen . . . Anne's voice, rising in agitation. Her mother's voice was lower, but also agitated. Kate couldn't hear the words either of them spoke, but she didn't have to know the cause of the dispute to be upset. Her mother and Anne never quarreled!

She had to know what was going on. While Carrie exhorted a contestant to spin the wheel again—"Go! Go!"—Kate walked to the kitchen. She wouldn't eavesdrop, she'd simply stroll into the room, pretending it was like any other evening and she was there to help prepare dinner.

She needn't have pretended anything. Her mother and Anne faced each other, faces pale and strained, seemingly unaware that Kate had entered the kitchen.

"No, Anne, it wouldn't be proper," Mrs. Fleming said. "You could fly up to San Francisco for a day, but I'd want you back that evening. I don't want you to spend the weekend up there."

"It costs too much to fly up for one day. And we wouldn't have enough time together. Please, Mother, I'm nineteen!"

"Are you telling me you're of legal age and you'll do what you want to whether I like it or not?"

"No, of course not! You know I didn't mean that. I'm just pointing out that I'm old enough to be trusted. I've promised I wouldn't stay in Larry's apartment, that I'll stay with Joan."

Kate had tiptoed to the sink. She stood, glass in hand, the other hand on the water tap, while a silence fell between her mother and sister. Was her mother going to give in? She hoped so with all her heart. Anne needed to see Larry so badly . . . surely her mother could see that. And how could she deny her when Anne was so good—almost an angel?

At last the mother spoke. "If you want to go so badly, Anne, I won't forbid you. You might think of the example you'll be setting for your sisters, though." She sighed heavily. "If you go through with this I'll be very disappointed in you, and Daddy will feel just as badly."

"Oh, Mom, you know I don't want to disappoint you, or hurt Daddy. And I certainly don't want to set a bad example for the other girls. I—I'll wait to see Larry until he comes home for the holidays."

Kate faced the sink. As she at last filled the water glass she heard a rush of footsteps and knew that Anne and her mother were embracing.

"That's my good girl. I knew you'd see it my way, Anne."

That night at the dinner table Anne calmly told about her day at Community College. She'd got an A on a Spanish test. She didn't mention that her heart had been broken. Kate had sometimes envied her older sister her goodness. Now she wasn't so sure she'd want to be that good.

Mrs. Fleming laughed rather self-consciously when she told her husband that Kate wanted her to offer her needlepoint for sale.

Mr. Fleming looked at his middle daughter. "If I had your head for business I'd own the telephone company by now instead of just being a supervisor."

Everyone laughed, but no one as heartily as Kate. She'd never been praised by her parents the way Anne so often was, and seldom punished as Carrie sometimes was . . . with subsequent babying. But at last she'd received some recognition, and she felt so good about it that for a while she forgot to worry about what kind of impression she'd make on Mrs. Barrows the following day.

9

Somehow the day passed. She'd dressed carefully that morning, wearing a green plaid skirt, with a neat white blouse which she'd kept in pristine condition by eating lunch very carefully, and not brushing up against anything, not even her seatback. Before going to the parking lot where she and Ross had agreed to meet, she went to the rest room and brushed her hair, coaxing the ends under in a short pageboy. She was tempted to put on a bit of eyeliner, but resisted. Her wide gray eyes were startling enough against her dark hair, she thought, without emphasizing them further. Ross had said he liked the combination, but no telling what his mother would think. She could imagine her saying, "Couldn't you find a normal-looking girl, Ross?" She settled for a dash of rose-colored lipstick, and ran to the parking lot.

Even then she'd fussed too long. The lot was half-empty when she reached it. Ross stood beside the Mustang, and made a hurrying motion when he saw her. Stan was at the wheel of the station wagon, impatiently gunning the motor.

"I'm sorry I'm late. I—"

"Let's go," Ross said, and got behind the wheel, leaving Kate to scamper around to the other side and climb in by herself, although he usually held the door for her.

It's not like me to be late, she wanted to say. I'm almost never late. But he wasn't interested in explanations. He drove as fast as the law allowed, out of the parking lot, and toward the foothills, the station wagon right behind him. He seemed almost like a stranger. Was he angry with her for being a few minutes late, or was he simply getting in the mood for the coming rehearsal? She'd noticed this about the group. They were tense and irritable before playing. Everything bothered them. But once they got into the music it claimed them completely, lifted them out of themselves . . . then, later, came the need to unwind.

For the first time it struck her that they might drink beer during or after the rehearsal. Perhaps the Barrows were such sophisticated people they didn't mind Ross and his friends drinking.

The streets became wider, the houses larger, the landscaping more lavish. At last the Mustang turned into the driveway of a big, Spanish-type house with a red-tiled roof. Bougainvillea spilled over the wrought-iron railing of an upstairs balcony. Kate had never been in such a house, but she decided she would not be intimidated by a building. The minute the car stopped she jumped out and went back to greet the others as they piled out of the station wagon.

"I'm glad you could come," Tamara told her.

She seemed to mean it. Perhaps being the only girl in the group she liked to have another girl around. It would be nice if they could become friends, Kate thought.

Ross led the way into a large tiled entrance hall. "Anybody home?" he called.

A woman came from the back of the house. She was tall, very trim, and she wore pants and a top made in the new sweatshirt material. Kate concluded at a glance that Mrs. Barrows would always wear the latest thing, dress her hair in the latest style, and have the newest gadgets in her kitchen.

Smiling, Mrs. Barrows said, "You knew I'd be here, Ross." Then looking around the group, "Hi, gang." Her eyes, not quite as dark a blue as Ross's, came to rest on Kate.

"I don't believe I know this young lady."

"That's right, I guess you've never met Kate," Ross said easily. *How could he not know what this meeting meant to both his mother and Kate? Boys!*

"This is Kate Fleming, Mom. Kate, this is my mother Phyllis Barrows."

The woman's eyes were slightly narrowed. "Do you play or sing, Kate?"

I don't do anything. But perhaps Mrs. Barrows knew that, could tell by looking at her. Was she deliberately trying to embarrass her because she'd decided she wasn't the kind of girl she wanted her son to run around with?

I'll show her I'm not the blah sort of girl she thinks I am. She struck a pose, hands clasped together, an exaggeratedly dreamy look on her face. *Carrie's face.*

"I'm just a groupie, I'm afraid. I can't play or sing, but I *adore* those who can. Who's the best little groupie in the world?" she asked as she looked at the circle of faces.

Everyone laughed, and there was a murmur of "You are," but Ross's laugh rang hollowly, as if he were embarrassed. Mrs. Barrows seemed amused, though.

"Musicians need their groupies," she said. "Now you young people go downstairs and start practicing. I want you to be through before Ken gets home." The gold bracelets on her arm jangled as she waved toward a door down the hall.

The door led to a large modern kitchen—gleaming copper, hanging plants, gadgets without number—to still another door that led to a basement.

The basement was cold after the heat outside, but nobody seemed to mind. Ross's drums were already set up, and there was a piano where Stan tried out a few chords.

"Why don't you have this thing tuned, man?"

"After our next paying gig," Ross said. "Now shut up, and let's get started. What are we going to do today, Oren?"

"We'll start with a little country," Oren said as he plugged in his guitar, "then work ourselves into some rock. You come in whenever you like, Tam."

"Yes, boss."

They were all so easy with each other . . . and with everyone else. Tamara had greeted Mrs. Barrows by her first name as casually as if she were talking to another girl. Why was she so awkward, so self-conscious, so unsure of herself, Kate wondered, that under stress she invariably adopted the personality of one of her sisters? What had Mrs. Barrows thought of her Carrie impersonation? She'd seemed amused, but what if she'd assumed that she was a clown, by nature, and expected her to keep it up?

She was cold. It was such a nice day she hadn't even worn a sweater to school. The boys began to perspire as they played, and Tamara's face was moist-looking after she'd belted out a medley of country songs. Kate looked around, but there was nothing she could wrap herself in. She would have hugged herself to keep warm if she hadn't been afraid it would attract Ross's attention. If they all had to stop playing while he found her a sweater they'd begin to think she was an awful drag—if they didn't already.

At last Oren said, "Intermission time!"

"I'll get some refreshments," Ross said. He held out a hand to Kate. "Want to make yourself useful?"

They went up the steep flight of stairs, into the kitchen. Mrs. Barrows was there wearing an apron that said, "The World's Greatest Chef."

"I'm making some sandwiches, dear," she told Ross. "And there's plenty of Coke in the fridge."

"I thought we'd drink beer," Ross said, but it was clear he was teasing his mother, and she responded accordingly.

"You'll do no such thing. I can't control what you do when you're out, but when you're around me you'll stick to soft drinks until you and your friends are of legal age."

As Ross laughed and opened the refrigerator door Kate wondered about Mrs. Barrows' values. She didn't seem to mind if Ross drank, just so she didn't know about it. . . . But perhaps that was a more reasonable attitude than to wring a promise from kids that would make them miserable if they kept it, and guilt-ridden if they didn't.

"I'll carry some of the Cokes," Kate offered.

"Why don't you let Ross take them down, and you stay here and help me finish the sandwiches?" Mrs. Barrows said.

"Why—sure." Kate wasn't fooled. Mrs. Barrows wanted to talk to her alone, to "get acquainted" was probably the way she thought of it. Awkwardly Kate moved to the counter where several kinds of bread and sandwich makings were laid out. She started to ask, "What can I do?" Then, with an unexpected burst of self-confidence she simply went ahead. "Suppose I spread mayonnaise on the white bread, mustard on the rye and whole wheat?" she said.

"Why, yes, that would be fine."

Kate washed her hands at the sink, found a hand towel in the cabinet below, and rummaged through a drawer until she found a knife. As she spread the bread Mrs. Barrows put on meat or cheese. With the team effort the platters soon began to fill up.

"You must be a big help to your mother," Mrs. Barrows observed.

"Well, I have an older sister who helps Mom the most, but—I guess I do my share."

The woman changed the subject to something that was of much more importance to her. "I'm so glad Ross brought you to the house. I knew he was seeing a new girl, and I've been anxious to meet you, but boys can be so thoughtless."

Kate laughed, her spirits soaring. What she'd feared would be a painful interlude was going better than she'd dreamed it could. Imagine her and Ross's mother laughing together over his thoughtlessness! She could hear Mrs. Barrows querying her son in the future. "Where is that nice girl you brought home not long ago? Kate. We had a lovely talk."

Suddenly the back door burst open. "It's only me!" Lela caroled. "I heard the kids practicing and I thought I'd—why—Kate—I didn't know you were here."

Yes, you did, Kate thought. You either knew I was coming, or you saw me get out of the car. How far away do you live—one or two doors?

"I'm surprised you came over when you knew Ross was practicing," Mrs. Barrows said. "You know you won't get much attention from him."

She doesn't like Lela, Kate thought. Then Mrs. Barrows smiled and said, "As long as you're here I'm going to put you to work. You can carry that bowl of chips downstairs."

"Sure, Phyl."

Of course Mrs. Barrows liked Lela. She'd known her all her life and she had no illusions about her, but that didn't mean she disliked her. She and Lela could have been mother and daughter, both tall, slim and style conscious. Both had blue eyes and blonde hair, although the gold in the older woman's hair had undoubtedly come from a bottle.

"I'll carry the sandwiches, Kate. You can bring the olives and pickles," Mrs. Barrows said as she started downstairs. "Kate helped me make the sandwiches, or they wouldn't be ready yet. Your timing, as usual, was perfect," she told Lela.

They both laughed, understanding each other.

The boys and Tamara shouted approval at sight of the food. As Mrs. Barrows went forward to put the platters of sandwiches on a long table in the center of the room Lela hung back and spoke to Kate with a taunting smile.

"So you're mother's little helper, are you? A lot of good it did you. I hope you don't think anyone is impressed by your little helpful homemaker act." Before Kate could more than draw in her breath Lela crossed to the table, bearing the bowl of potato chips aloft. "Tada!" she cried, making a big deal of serving the chips.

"What are you doing here?" Ross asked her none-too-cordially.

"I came over to feed you some potato chips." And she crammed one in his mouth.

He couldn't resist the game . . . or maybe he didn't want to. Laughing, he stuffed a potato chip in her mouth. In the meantime Mrs. Barrows said, "Well, enjoy, kids," and went upstairs. Kate took a paper plate, put some food on it, and slid onto one of the benches. When Ross and Lela had finished their game they sat down on the opposite bench.

Kate felt out of place, unnecessary. Why had Ross brought her here? Why was he playing games with Lela, sitting beside her? After a moment she realized she was being unreasonable. Why hadn't she been the one to start the game with him? Why hadn't she sat beside him before Lela had a chance to? Why wasn't she laughing and talking like the others? It was her fault, not Ross's, that she didn't fit in. After a while he looked across the table at her.

"You okay, Kate? You're not eating much."

All eyes were on her, and her heaped plate. Why had she taken so much food? "I guess my eyes were bigger than my stomach," she said. Grinning, she put her fingers to her eyes and distended them as far as she could. She'd once seen Carrie do that when she'd been scolded for taking too much food.

The ripple of laughter that ran around the table was restrained. Only Stan seemed amused.

"You're quite a cut-up, Kate," he said. "Maybe you could work up a little comedy routine and do it when we play our gigs. What do you think, Ross? Wouldn't you like to have your girl in the act?"

"No!" Ross all but shouted. "Kate is a businesswoman, not a comedian."

"A businesswoman?" Tamara said. "What kind of business, Kate?"

"Oh, I have sort of a babysitting agency. It's nothing —just something to do until I can get a real job." It *was* nothing to these talented kids. She felt like kicking Ross under the table for bringing it up. And now that he had, and she'd been drawn into explaining about it, he wasn't even helping her out. He was watching her in frowning silence.

"It sounds interesting to me," Tamara said. "If I weren't so wrapped up in singing I'd want to do something like that—perform a real service."

Tamara was on *her* side. And Lela knew it.

"What's the matter with you kids?" she cried. "You all sound so stuffy. I can't imagine what's got into you. You didn't used to be like this. Hey, I've got an idea. Why don't you all come over to my place when you're through practicing? My folks are away, and I'll give the housekeeper the rest of the day off. We can play records and dance." Laughing, she added, "In fact, we can do just about anything we want to. Oh, you're invited, too—Kate." By making the last remark she made it plain she didn't consider Kate part of the gang.

It was Ross who vetoed the idea. "I've got to study for those exams that are coming up."

When the others made similar excuses Lela stood up. "If you people don't want to have any fun I guess I'll call Hank and a few other kids . . . see you." She got up and walked away from the table not bothering to take her dishes with her.

I helped to make the sandwiches, I'll be darned if I'll do the cleaning up, Kate vowed. *So you're mother's little helper, are you?* Lela had taunted her. And gone on to say it wouldn't do her any good.

A thought struck Kate like a bolt of lightning. When she and Ross had sat in the orange grove he'd said he didn't know what he wanted to do with his life; he might do some odd-ball thing like running a bait shop on the coast, or scratching out a living with some cabins in the desert. He ended by saying that he might be a realtor like his dad, but that was an afterthought. The important thing was that he'd never confided his uncertainty to Lela, or she would't have made that remark about his wife not having to be a kitchen drudge.

She felt so good realizing that Ross had shared something with her he hadn't shared with Lela that when the others offered to help clean up she said, "No, you get back to your playing. It'll take me only a minute to clear the table."

Actually, she had to make three trips up and down the steep flight of stairs before the table was clean. There was no sign of Mrs. Barrows so she wrapped the leftovers and put them in the fridge. She was putting the empty cans and other refuse in a brown paper bag when her smug pleasure over Ross confiding his secret thoughts to her suddenly drained away. Maybe he hadn't talked to Lela about bait shops on the coast, or tourist cabins in the desert, because he knew it was just adolescent daydreaming—knew Lela would laugh at him and tell him to grow up. She left the bag of refuse in the sink and went downstairs.

The second practice session was short. Everyone had to get to their homework. They trooped upstairs, and were in the front hall when Mr. Barrows came home. He was tall and good-looking, but Kate thought his rusty-brown hair, flecked with gray, was unusually long for a man his age. He clapped the boys on the shoulders, and flirted with Kate when Ross made the introduction.

"I like your folks," she said when they were in the car.

"Yeah, they're all right." He glanced sideways. "I

don't know what Mom thought when you made that remark about being a groupie, though. Is that the way you feel, Kate?''

"No!" she gasped. "My liking you has nothing to do with—"

"Then why did you say such a thing?"

"I don't know. I was sort of clowning, I guess. Do I always have to be serious?"

"No, but—something else puzzled me. You said your babysitting business was nothing. I thought you took it pretty seriously."

Feeling cornered, she flared up. "Why are you picking apart every little thing I said? If I can't be myself—"

"Sometimes it seems to me you're not being yourself. But let's drop it for now."

She didn't want to drop it. She wanted to explain, but she didn't know how. He'd think she was a mental case if she told him she sometimes took on the personalities of her sisters because she seemed to have no identity of her own—that if she relied on her own personality she'd say things out of sheer self-consciousness that she didn't mean. Like saying that her babysitting business was nothing.

"Okay, we'll drop it," she mumbled.

When he dropped her off, it was with the parting she'd hoped was over between them.

"See you."

10

A bell rang when Kate opened the door of Ye Gift Shoppe. Mrs. LaCross smiled at her from behind the counter.

"What can I do for you, Kate?"

She was a young woman who Kate knew had two small children. They were in nursery school during the day, but if she went out in the evening she called on Kate for a sitter.

"I want to show you something." Kate marched briskly to the counter, opened a tissue-wrapped package, and spread out several pieces of her mother's needlepoint; a chair cover, a sampler that said God Bless Our Home, the basket of violets and several other pieces. "My mother does this work," she said. "I'd like to put these pieces here on consignment."

The woman studied the needlepoint critically, as if looking for flaws, but apparently she didn't find any. "I haven't much space left," she said, "but this really is lovely work. Would your mother be satisfied with a sixty-forty split? She'd get the sixty, of course."

"Seventy-thirty," Kate said, although she'd had no idea of what kind of split would be offered. She could always back down.

The woman laughed. "You have quite a business head on your shoulders. All right, seventy-thirty."

The rest of the details were quickly worked out, and Kate rushed home. It was Saturday, and the day before a telephone had been installed in her room, along with an answering machine. Her mother was so tired of taking her calls when she wasn't there that she'd given in with only a brief argument. "As long as you're paying for it I guess I can't object," she'd finally said.

Kate was thrilled when she found that the machine had already recorded a message. She immediately dialed the number. "Hello, Mrs. Bradley. This is Kate's Dependable Babysitting Service."

A few minutes later she called Doris. "I have a job for you for tonight."

"Gee, I can't sit tonight, Kate. Jeff is coming over and we're going to try some dance steps. We're going to the Halloween dance at the Community Center. You and Ross are coming, aren't you?"

"I don't know," Kate said. "Right now I'm looking for a sitter for the Bradleys. You were supposed to be on call tonight."

"I meant to be, but Jeff just called and said he wanted to come over." Her voice fell. "I think I'm in love, Kate."

The announcement came as no surprise, but Kate pretended it did. "That's wonderful, Doris. I bet he's in love with you, too, or soon will be." There were no complications here. Both grew up in the same neighborhood, had the same family background, the same values.

"Thanks, Kate. How are you and Ross getting along?"

"All right," she said shortly. She had no time for a gab session even if she could have answered Doris's question in either a positive or negative way. How *are* Ross and I getting along? "About tonight," she said. "You'd better call Jeff back and tell him you're sitting."

"But, Kate—"

"I'm sorry, Doris. I have to have girls I can depend on."

"You mean you won't give me any more jobs if I don't sit tonight?"

It was tough being a businesswoman. She knew how her friend felt. *Would I put business before spending an evening with Ross?* Yes, if I had to.

"You agreed to be on call," she said. "Take the job or I'll pull your card out of the file."

"Darn you, Kate! You have no heart!" Then grudgingly, "Okay, I'll sit."

Kate stayed in her room most of the day, taking calls, assigning girls to jobs near their homes whenever possible, always making sure they'd get a ride home if they didn't have their own transportation. When she wasn't on the phone she worked on her filing system and bookkeeping. She kept hoping Ross would call. He'd never called her, and it made her wonder if he thought of her at all when they were apart. She thought of him constantly. No matter what she was doing some part of her mind was on him. In her idle moments she carried on long conversations with him on every topic under the sun . . . movies, books, politics, religion . . .

He didn't call, and she spent the evening watching television with her parents and Carrie. Anne stayed in her room, pleading homework, but Kate thought she was more likely daydreaming about Larry. Kate still thought she should have insisted on visiting him, and had definitely decided she was glad she wasn't as "good" as her older sister.

Sunday Carrie had her way. The family outing was to Disneyland. It was compensation for not being allowed to date, but Kate thought it was a poor trade-off for Carrie. She frequently cried, "I'm tired of being treated like a baby! I bet you'll never let me date!"

Were the parents clinging to her because she was the youngest child, their baby? Yet as Carrie went from Frontierland to Fantasy Land, eyes bright, sometimes clapping her hands in childish delight, Kate thought her parents were probably right. Carrie was young for her age, maybe not ready to date.

Anne was quiet, her smiles rather absentminded. Kate had a feeling the family was changing, that it was not the same as it had been even a few weeks ago. Did Carrie's childish exuberance mask a growing rebellion? Anne was more now than her parents' adored oldest daughter. She was a woman in love.

And I, what am I? Kate wondered if she was really in love with Ross or did she just have a crush on him because he was so handsome, so exciting? She was convinced now that he wasn't using her to make Lela jealous. He wouldn't do anything so cruel. But perhaps he knew Lela was wrong for him, and was trying to get over her by going with Kate. If he really cared for her wouldn't they have become closer by now? He'd all but said that she was his girl, but he'd never told her how he felt about her—he never called her at home.

"You're quiet, Kate," her father said. They'd walked on by themselves when the others had stopped, waiting for Carrie to take pictures of the parade of Disney characters on her new Polaroid.

"I'm okay, Dad. I—was just thinking."

"Thinking about what?"

If she told him about her doubts of herself, and of Ross's feelings toward her, perhaps he would reassure her. If he told her she was pretty, and Ross was a lucky fellow to have her as his girl friend, maybe she'd feel pretty and desirable—and act it. That would make a difference in how Ross felt about her. She knew it.

"I was just thinking about—" she began, not sure exactly what she was going to say. But then it didn't matter, as Carrie came running forward, waving a handful of Polaroid prints. The father's face lit up.

"Let's see, young one. Say, these are really something. You're quite a photographer."

As the school year advanced, Kate had to buckle down to some serious studying. And with her babysitting business keeping her busy, as well, she had little time to mope because she saw so little of Ross. He was on the track team, and between that and his music and studies, he explained that he'd have to take it easy on dating for a while.

"I understand," Kate said. And was glad she could add, "I'm pretty busy, too." Independent Kate. It was funny how she tried to live up to her mother's description of her.

One day when she went home, expecting one of her mother's usual greetings, she got a surprise.

"Guess what?" Mrs. Fleming said.

"Daddy's run off with another woman."

"Kate! What a thing to joke about. Guess again and be serious this time."

Kate could think of only one thing that would bring

111

such a sparkle to her mother's eyes, but she didn't want to spoil her surprise by guessing it.

"I give up. Tell me."

"I sold the basket of violets. A lady paid thirty dollars for it."

"Oh, Mom, that's great!" She wanted to run and hug her mother the way Carrie or Anne would do, but she had the feeling her mother didn't expect a display of affection from her.

"I've already started a basket of wildflowers. Maybe that will be my—theme."

Carrie burst through the door a moment later. When she heard the news she predictably hugged and kissed her mother.

"You're like an artist—just think." Then her thoughts immediately turned to herself. "I can paint pictures pretty good. Maybe I'll be a real artist."

In her room Kate studied herself in the mirror, seeking a clue as to what she would be. If she could only define the kind of person she was she could set goals for herself, wouldn't feel as if she might go off in any direction. What kind of role would she be cast in if she were an actress? Probably as a businesswoman in wide-shouldered suits like Joan Crawford used to wear . . . maybe not even that. She'd more likely be cast in bit parts, one of the people in a crowd scene.

When the telephone rang she reached for a pencil and pad, thinking it was someone wanting a babysitter. But it was Ross. She'd never heard his voice over the phone before, but she knew it at once. It was so deep it was a bit gravelly, yet soft, too, and the intimacy of it, speaking right into her ear, was almost more exciting than being with him.

"We haven't been able to see much of each other lately, so I thought we might talk awhile."

It was a dream come true. He did miss her when they weren't together. Oh, how wonderful to know it wasn't as one-sided as she sometimes thought.

"Sure," she said, stretching the extension cord to the limit so she could lie back against her bed pillows, feeling luxurious and a bit sensual. "How's everything?" she asked.

"The track coach can't decide if I'm a sprinter or a distance runner, so he's putting me in the middle distance races."

She laughed. "As a middle sister I know exactly how you feel. I'm always in between, too."

"You're like the sandwich filling, you mean." His tone was light, bantering.

"Or a third bookend," she said.

"Not that. There's no need for a third bookend."

I know. But her voice bubbled as she said, "Okay, I'm not a third bookend. I'm the filling in the sandwich if you say so."

They talked some more, and she had no trouble keeping up her end of the light conversation. Over the phone it seemed she could speak naturally, with no self-consciousness, no need to borrow one of her sister's personalities. Finally, when she sensed he was about to hang up, she asked the question she'd been wanting to ask him for a long time.

"Could you have dinner with us some night?"

"Sure. I'd like to. Want to set a date?"

She started to say, Whenever's convenient for you, but changed it to, "Would Thursday night be all right?"

"This is Tuesday . . . yeah, Thursday night would be great. What time do you want me there?"

"We sit down at six-thirty."

He chuckled, the sound waves tickling her ear. "I

113

remember. That's why you couldn't go to The Pump that afternoon. The family dinner is a big thing at your house, you said. I think that's nice, Kate."

"I guess so," she said. She wished he hadn't mentioned The Pump. What if he casually mentioned drinking beer Thursday night, explaining that his parents didn't mind as long as they didn't know about it?

He wouldn't. Why was she borrowing trouble, already worrying about Thursday night? She was proud of him, proud of her family. It would be a wonderful evening. And once he'd visited in her home there'd be a new closeness between them.

"Well, I'd better let you go," he said. "See you."

She hugged the phone to her before hanging up. She wasn't worried about the "See you," anymore. It was just a phrase he used. Most likely he used it with Lela, too.

Why had she thought of Lela? *You can't bear to be happy, can you?* But she'd risked something in asking him to her house. She was involving her family, letting them know how serious she was about him. Anne had asked only one boy to dinner before she'd started to go with Larry. She no longer doubted that Ross was interested in her, but Lela was still a part of his life. They were neighbors. Lela could run into his house, make herself at home—golden-haired Lela with the lavender eyes, and the sylph-like figure that was made to wear expensive clothes . . . a girl like his mother. Wasn't that what boys looked for when they were ready to settle down?

That evening she told the family that she'd invited Ross to dinner Thursday night. She wished she could ask her mother to prepare something special but she didn't dare. Larry had always taken pot luck, and just because he was a neighborhood boy and Ross lived in Foothill Estates she couldn't ask that he be treated like visiting royalty.

"Looks like it's getting serious," her father said. His smile was teasing, but his eyes were probing.

Her mother said, "He knows we sit down at six-thirty, doesn't he?" She seemed to have been expecting the announcement.

"Maybe he thinks we drink champagne with dinner," Carrie said, and mimicked holding a champagne glass aloft.

Anne gave her gentle laugh and said, "So he'll find out that we peasants drink milk or coffee."

Mrs. Fleming served chicken and dumplings Thursday night. Ross ate two helpings and said he'd never tasted anything better in his life.

"I hope you've taught Kate to cook like this, Mrs. Fleming," he said. Then turned beet-red. Everybody laughed, but in a way that eased his embarrassment. Anne, bless her, jumped in and changed the subject to further spare him.

"I've heard you may go to San Francisco State, Ross."

"Yes, I most likely will."

"My fiancé goes there."

It was the first time Anne had referred to Larry as her fiancé, and her parents exchanged glances that Kate interpreted as, So they've made up their minds. Anne and Larry talked on the phone every weekend. Absence must have made their hearts grow fonder. . . .

"Would you like milk or coffee, Ross?" Mrs. Fleming asked.

"Coffee, please."

Kate took coffee, too. She was not forbidden to

drink it, although her mother preferred her to drink milk. There was peach pie for dessert, and again Ross took two helpings.

When Kate started to help clear the table both her mother and Anne told her they could manage without her.

Carrie said loudly, "Then I get out of doing the dishes, too, when my boyfriend comes to dinner!"

"Bet you haven't got a boyfriend," Ross said with a teasing smile.

"No, but I will have if my mother ever decides I'm old enough to date. She treats me like I'm ten," Carrie complained.

As they left the dining room Ross asked Kate if she'd like to go for a ride.

"Love to. I'll get a sweater." She spoke lightly, but she was worried about where he'd want to go—perhaps to The Pump or some other place where there was drinking. Even though he'd enjoyed the meal with her family he might want to finish the evening doing something more exciting.

When they got in the car he seemed to have no particular destination in mind. He drove slowly, commenting on what a nice family she had. "Everybody isn't so lucky."

Kate wondered if he was thinking of himself. No, she thought, his mother wasn't as domestic as hers, but she didn't seem to neglect her family. Perhaps he was thinking of Lela, whose parents thought nothing of leaving her on her own. He'd mentioned once that Lela had been neglected in some ways, overindulged in others.

He stopped the car at the side of the road just at the edge of town. It was a balmy evening with a harvest moon hanging up in the sky like a giant orange balloon.

He dropped an arm around Kate's shoulders. Then he spoke her name, softly, tentatively.

"Kate?"

She turned to him, and almost as spontaneously as they'd kissed in the orange grove that day they kissed again. Her hands lightly touched his shoulders while his arms settled around her, holding her loosely. His lips were warm and sweetly seeking.

It was perhaps a second or two, maybe three, when she realized the kiss should end. Only who should end it? He should, because he'd started it, she thought. But he didn't end it, and she decided he was waiting for her to draw away. She was reluctant to do so, fearing he'd think she was rejecting him. What would another girl do? Did other girls have an instinct that guided them, an instinct that she lacked?

All she lacked was self-confidence. If she were Anne she'd end the kiss gracefully, drawing back her lips and smiling for a moment to show she'd found the kiss pleasurable. Carrie would give him a push away and say, "A person has to breathe once in a while, you know."

And in the end that's what she did. She pushed at his shoulders, took a big gulp of air and said, "A person has to breathe once in a while, you know."

She could have bit her tongue the minute the words were out. They would have sounded all right if Carrie had said them, but coming from her they sounded harsh and critical. All at once she knew he'd been waiting for her to end the kiss simply because it was the girl who was supposed to. And she'd made it sound as if he'd been forcing himself on her.

There was a grim silence as he turned to the wheel without a word. He drove faster now, as if he couldn't wait to get her home. She tried to think of something to say that would make things right, but she was too miserable to think rationally.

When he stopped in front of her house he turned to her, trying to force some warmth into his voice as he thanked her for the meal.

"I was glad you could come." Then impulsively she leaned toward him and pressed a quick kiss on his lips. She liked him, liked his kisses, and she wouldn't let him drive off thinking she didn't.

"Wow!" he said. "I don't know what that was for, but I sure liked it." He spoke anxiously now. "If I got out of line before—"

"You didn't. I'm just not used to kissing, and I wasn't sure how to act."

He nodded, understanding in his eyes. "A guy doesn't always know how to act, either." He took her hand and wrapped his big hand around it. "You're some special kind of girl, Kate. I mean, being honest about your feelings, kissing me like that."

"You're special, too. Now I'd better go in before Carrie stares holes through the curtains."

He looked at the house and laughed. "I think I do see a little nose pressed against the window."

As she ran up the path she could have hugged herself. Kissing him on impulse, confessing she'd goofed before because she was inexperienced with boys, had magically rescued the evening. Sometimes I do something right, in spite of myself, she thought.

11

The Music Makers were to play for the Halloween Dance at the Community Center. This time Ross offered to pick Kate up if she didn't mind getting there early. "I don't mind at all," she said.

More and more lately she'd been trusting her feelings, speaking her true thoughts. She didn't know if being his girl had given her more self-confidence, if it came from her success in business, or what. But it was good to express herself freely and naturally. And when she did Ross always seemed pleased.

"That's my girl," he said, giving her a quick hug when she told him she didn't mind being at the dance early.

She enjoyed watching him set up his drums, hearing the first strains of music as Oren tuned his guitar. And then the full swell of the amplified sound as the others came in. She sat at a table that had been reserved for the group just to one side of the bandstand, and watched the hall fill up. The crowd was about the same as it had been before, most of the kids in their early teens, some who probably couldn't afford the price of

119

other entertainment. Doris and Jeff came in, waved, and immediately went onto the floor, where they swung into the motions of the latest dance.

The Center was decorated with orange and black streamers, black cats and plastic pumpkins. A nicely decorated refreshment table was set up against one wall. Kate was thinking how festive it all looked when a familiar, high-pitched voice assaulted her eardrums.

"Hi. Mind if Hank and I sit down?"

Lela didn't wait for an answer. She pulled out a chair and sat down, impatiently motioning for Hank to do the same.

"It says 'Reserved,'" the big football player said, pointing to a hand-lettered sign on the table.

"What's the difference? It's probably reserved for Ross and the other musicians. And they certainly won't mind my sitting here."

Hank sat down carefully on the small chair as if he feared it would collapse under his weight. He wore his football sweater over casual clothes, but Lela was dressed in a misty green gown with a low neckline. She'd played up her narrow, uptilted eyes with a careful makeup job, and enhanced the thin line of her lips with a mauve lipgloss. . . . Kate had worn jeans and a turtleneck sweater as the hall was kept cool for the dancers. She'd worn no makeup except a dash of coral lipstick that matched her sweater, as she didn't think a made-up look went well with jeans.

"These affairs are an awful drag, aren't they?" Lela observed. "Or do you find them exciting, a—Kate?"

Somehow Kate was not intimidated by the other girl. *She's not a nice person. Why should I let her bother me?*

"I enjoy hearing the group play. And I like to see the kids dance and have a good time. Most of them probably can't afford disco's, or giving private parties."

"Good grief, a bleeding heart! Now I know what Ross sees in you. He's always feeling sorry for some loser." She waved a mauve-taloned hand at the crowd. "They wouldn't be so hard up if their parents weren't too lazy to work. It makes my dad furious that we have to support places like this with our taxes."

Kate felt her heart pumping wildly, and was trying to find the right words to express her indignation when the set ended. Ross was first to reach the table.

"Hi, there," he said, nodding at Hank. Then to Lela, "What are you doing here? I thought you were going to that new disco over in Oakdale."

"We are," Lela replied, giving no sign of being hurt at Ross's less than enthusiastic greeting. "But first I thought it would be fun to do a little slumming. This is a pretty dreary scene, isn't it?"

"I don't see anything dreary about it," Ross snapped.

Stan brought up some more chairs, and everyone crowded in at the table. Soft drinks were brought, but Lela made a face after testing hers.

"It isn't spiked. Hasn't anybody got a bottle?"

"We're working—remember?" Ross said.

Lela turned to Hank. "Haven't you got a bottle?"

"Heck, no. I'm in training."

Lela gave him a disgusted look and pushed aside her Coke. "I'll have a real drink when we get to Oakdale." She put her hand on Ross's arm as if she were claiming a piece of baggage. "Let's dance," she said.

Ross was hot and flushed from his exertions on the bandstand, and he'd barely tasted his Coke, but he gave a little shrug and got to his feet. As the couple danced off Lela called to Hank, "Don't just sit there—ask Kate to dance."

Hank sprang up as if Lela had jerked a string that controlled him. Kate wasn't eager to dance with him, but she didn't want to hurt his feelings. Besides, it was probably better to dance than to sit there and watch Ross and Lela on the floor. They looked so good together, both so tall and graceful. And they danced together with the ease of long practice. That was the key to their relationship, Kate thought. They'd known each other forever, had probably learned to dance together . . . learned to kiss and touch. That was why Ross couldn't be angry with Lela for long. . . .

Hank was not nearly so much at home on the dance floor as he was on the football field. Kate finally gave up trying to match his rhythm and they swayed to the music, not touching.

"I haven't danced much," he confessed when his big feet got tangled up.

"Really?" Kate asked with suppressed laughter.

"Honest. I've gone in more for sports. But now, going with Lela, I've got to learn a lot of other things. I've got to make some money, too. It's expensive to go to disco's and places like that."

"I suppose it is."

She'd thought that Hank came from Lela's neighborhood, even though he was a diamond in the rough. She wouldn't have pursued the matter, though, if he hadn't seemed anxious to talk . . . did Lela ever listen to him? He was one of six children, he told Kate. The family had come to California as migrant laborers. They were doing better now, living on a small farm outside of town.

"I'm going to try to get an athletic scholarship so I can go to college. That would sure make my folks proud." He shook his big, shaggy head. "I've got to do more studying, though . . . seems like I don't have time for it anymore."

And you won't have, Kate thought, as long as Lela decides she wants you as an escort. Lela dangled the football star on her arm as if he were an oversized charm.

Lela and Hank left when the dance ended. Kate was about to sit down at the table when Tamara asked her if she wanted to powder her nose.

"Sure," Kate said. She liked the other girl more all the time, and was glad they'd have a chance to talk.

"Thank goodness *she* cut out," Tamara said as they made their way down the hall to the rest room. "I'm just sorry for poor Hank. She doesn't care two cents about him. She's just trying to make Ross jealous—as if he were that dumb."

Kate didn't know what to say so she remained silent. Tamara shot her a knowing look.

"Don't like to gossip, huh? I admire you for that. But I'm not saying anything behind Lela's back I wouldn't say to her face. She likes to manipulate boys, and it makes me furious to see how glad most of them are to let her do it. Even Ross, as well as he knows her, jumps at her command . . . and the nerve of her, ordering Hank to dance with you just because she knows he looks terrible on the dance floor. While she and Ross were gliding along like swans she knew you'd be getting trampled on."

Kate laughed. "I fooled her. We didn't even try to dance. We just moved to the music and talked. He told me quite a bit about himself."

"You're that kind of girl," Tamara said, as she pushed open the rest room door. "I bet people are always confiding in you."

"Well—" She said no more, but she realized it was true. *Another quality I have. I'm interested in people, and show it, so they confide in me.*

She and Tamara freshened up, then went back to the hall where the boys were already warming up. Just before she ran up the steps leading to the bandstand Tamara said, "Listen, we're going to The Pump later, and while the boys guzzle beer we can talk. I only drink one or two beers, and I bet you're not much of a drinker, either."

"No, I—I'm not," Kate said through suddenly dry lips. She made her way back to the table that was still littered with paper cups. There was a mauve smudge on one. She wouldn't have dared to wear such a shade of lipstick, and she thought that symbolized the difference between her and the other girl in Ross's life. Lela was sophisticated. To drink or not to drink was simply not an issue with her . . . nor with Ross, either. So how could she tell him about her promise to her folks?

His mother had practically given him permission to drink, just so she didn't know about it. That attitude no doubt seemed right and reasonable to him. What he would consider unreasonable was a promise that would keep Kate from drinking even a sip of beer, under any circumstances. She could imagine his amazement—or would it be pitying amusement—if she told him of the promise her parents had wrung from her?

Well, now she'd have to tell him. There was no excuse she could possibly give for not going to The Pump. She'd used them all up.

There *was* a way out, of course. She could go to the tavern with the gang, take a few sips of beer, joke that she didn't want to drink too much for fear she'd get an H.O. Ross would laugh and say, "Smart girl. It's sure no fun to have a hangover." They'd click glasses, she'd drink perhaps half a glass of beer, and that would be that. Big problem solved.

No. It mustn't happen that way. *I don't want to be the kind of girl who breaks a solemn promise. I don't think I am that kind of girl.*

But she couldn't be sure.

She pushed the problem to the back of her mind. She'd deal with it when the time came. For now she'd lose herself in the beat of the music, let the amplified sound drown out all thought. Ross flirted with her as he beat a wild tattoo on the drums, reminding her she was his girl.

Reality returned when the last number ended. The hall soon emptied. Ross had stowed his drums in the station wagon, and come back to the table.

"Tam told you we were going to The Pump, didn't she?"

Kate nodded.

"It's all right, isn't it? You don't have to rush home?"

An out if she wanted to take it . . . but she didn't dare. How soon his bright smile would turn to a frown if she said she did have to rush home—if she gave any excuse at all for not joining him and his friends at the tavern that was their special place.

"No," she said in a strange sort of waking dream. "I don't have to rush home."

"Great!" He propelled her after the others who were rushing outside. He helped her into the Mustang and slammed the door.

"Here we go! Next stop The Pump!" She'd never seen him in such high spirits.

She didn't think ahead. She chattered volubly, almost convincing herself she was as excited as Ross.

"You've never been to The Pump?" he asked.

"No," she answered, an inflection in her voice that indicated it was just one of those places she'd somehow missed.

"You'll like it. The owner is an okay guy. He thinks I.D. stands for Intelligent Drinking."

He also makes money on serving teenage kids. But she said enthusiastically, "He sure does sound like an okay guy."

They drove perhaps five miles past the city limits, and followed the station wagon into a dirt parking lot beside a small, drab building that was faintly illuminated by a small string of neon lights. *The Pump.*

"So you made it, did you?" Stan called as Kate and Ross got out of the car. "We thought you might have stopped for some smooching."

"That comes later," Ross said, laughing louder than usual.

They walked to the door, and Oren opened it. It was so dark inside Kate could see nothing, but the others knew their way, and soon they were seated at a corner table.

"We keep a low profile in case 'The Law' should put in an appearance," Ross told Kate. "They never have, though, and they probably won't, as long as there's no trouble. So don't worry about it."

Kate could see better now. The place was small and dingy, with a bar running along one wall, cheap tables and chairs arranged around the other walls. Most of the people in the tavern were middle-aged; the couples at the tables, single men at the bar. A juke box was playing an old Dean Martin record, and a few couples were dancing although there was a sign over the juke box that said No Dancing, County Ordinance. The fleshy man behind the bar evidently didn't enforce the ordinance any more than he required ID's of his young customers.

"Five drafts, huh?" Ross said as the boys started to the bar. Laughing, "Nobody would rather have champagne?"

She could speak up and say jokingly, "Yes, I want champagne—I never drink anything else." And maybe she could stick to it, still making a joke of it, until finally saying, "All right, if I can't have champagne I'll have plain Coke." It was the nutty kind of thing they might think was funny.

"Just stop talking and go get the beer!" Tamara said. "Kate and I are dying of thirst, aren't we, Kate?"

Kate nodded. Tamara was a good girl. Drinking a couple of beers didn't make her bad. *Why should I be a social outcast just because my parents have outdated ideas?* Some parents would be *glad* to have their kids drink a little beer just so they stayed away from harder stuff. A promise she'd made before she was old enough to know what was involved was not binding. She'd drink a little beer, see how she liked it, see how it affected her. If she began to feel funny she wouldn't drink a drop more . . . blessed relief now that the decision had been made.

"Here you are, girls." The boys put the beer on the table together with a big bowl of pretzels. They sat down and Ross held up a slender Pilsner glass.

"Salute!" he said.

"*A la sante!*" Tamara toasted.

"Cheers!" Kate recognized her own voice although she was hardly aware of speaking.

Ross seemed pleased, and clicked his glass against hers. "Drink up. There's plenty more where this came from."

Kate started to put the glass to her lips, then set it

down on the table, instead. Her hands were trembling, and her heart was beating fast. It wasn't so easy to break a promise, after all, even one she'd been coerced into making. She knew she'd never feel quite right with herself again if she drank even a sip of beer.

She moved the glass to the edge of the table, and reached for a pretzel. As she did so the slender glass tipped over and the beer spilled over the table and onto her lap.

"Clumsy me!" she cried. "Look what I've done!"

Ross jumped up. "No harm done. I'll get a towel from the bar."

He was back in a second, and the beer was soon mopped up from the table. But Kate's jeans and sweater were soaked.

"I'll go to the rest room and sponge off so I won't smell like a brewery," she said.

"I'll have another beer waiting for you when you get back," Ross told her.

He started to the bar, but she caught his arm. "No, don't bother. I drank so much Coke at the dance I'm not a bit thirsty. Besides, I have a little headache. I think that's what made me so awkward. It's one of those dizzy headaches, and I'm afraid beer will make it worse."

She hurried to the rest room, feeling guilty because he looked so concerned. She spent as much time as she dared, sponging her clothes with wet paper towels. She was a soggy mess when she was through, and she still felt guilty over causing Ross concern. Yet overall, she felt good about herself. She hadn't broken her promise, and she'd got out of drinking the beer so adroitly that Ross wasn't put out with her. At the time she'd managed to convince herself that spilling the beer was an accident, but deep down she'd known it wasn't.

Back at the table Ross said, "You sure you don't want a beer?"

She shook her head. "I'll just munch on some pretzels. If I get thirsty I'll let you know."

Tamara drank two beers, the boys each drank three. They talked music, went over how they'd performed that night. Oren told Tamara he thought she'd forced her voice.

"You'd better watch it. Your voice is your instrument. You have to take care of it."

They all got a bit loud, but then Oren said, "Coffee time. You want a cup of coffee, Kate?"

"I'd love one."

And so the evening at The Pump ended. When he'd driven her home Ross kissed Kate's temples.

"That's to make your headache well." He lightly kissed her lips. "And that's because I like you a lot."

"Oh, Ross!" There was anguish in her cry, but he didn't hear it because he wasn't listening for it. He smiled, thinking the cry was her way of telling him she liked him, too.

She did, of course—oh, so much. But some day there'd be a showdown between them. Next time they went to The Pump she wouldn't dare spill her beer. If she told him the truth would he like her less? One thing she knew for sure now, if she broke her promise to her parents she wouldn't like herself at all.

12

The first two weeks of November flew by with Kate busier than she'd ever been in her life. There was the babysitting business, her studies, and then both she and Ross were asked to serve on the decoration committee for the Harvest Ball. That was the biggest event of the fall semester. A full dance band would play, and formal attire was in order, although it wasn't required.

It was Jaclyn Myers, president of the senior class who came up to Kate and Ross as they entered the cafeteria one day. She was a tall, attractive girl, a top scholar and active in all school affairs.

"Ross, you're just the man I'm looking for," she said, "I'm chairing the Harvest Ball committee, and we need some fellows to help decorate the gym. You'll help out, won't you?"

"Do I have any choice?" Ross asked with a grin.

"No, as a matter of fact you don't," Jaclyn answered with a laugh. "You've got by pretty easy as vice-president of the senior class. Sometimes the president dumps most of the work on the vice-president. You have to admit I haven't done that."

"No, you haven't," Ross said. Then, "Aren't you going to ask Kate to help out?"

Jaclyn looked at Kate. "Sure. We need girls, too. How about it, Kate?"

"I'd be glad to help."

"Good. We'll meet in the gym after school, and lay out our plans, although we won't be able to start decorating until after the game with Central High."

Kate was thrilled to be serving on a committee that was comprised mostly of seniors. She even made a suggestion that afternoon that was well-received. Why not hang oranges from the boughs that would decorate the gym? "Sort of a tribute to our name."

"Neat idea," Jaclyn said. "Everybody agree?"

Ross's "Yes!" was louder than anybody's.

Kate had missed the school bus, so Ross drove her home. She kept waiting for him to say something about them going to the dance together, but he didn't. Was it an oversight, or did he think she'd take it for granted they'd go as a couple? Or was it something entirely different? The ball was an important event. He'd want to take the girl he cared for the most. Asking Kate to tag along with The Music Makers and taking her to an occasional movie, was one thing . . . asking her to the Harvest Ball was an entirely different matter.

"How's that cute little sister of yours?" he asked. "Have your folks let her date yet?"

"No, but they let her take a babysitting job. I talked the Fletchers, some people I used to sit for, into giving her a chance. I think that may help the folks to see that she's growing up."

"Kids are usually more grown up than their parents realize. . . . I guess Anne is looking forward to her fiancé coming home for the holidays."

"Yes. It won't be long now."

"We're excited because Luke will be coming home from Stanford. It's nice to have the whole family together."

Was he talking so much because he didn't want to ask her to the ball, and he knew it was on her mind? He drew up in front of her house. "I'd better let you go in," he said. "See you."

"See you," she managed to answer. He *wasn't* going to ask her.

She was half out of the car when he said, "I thought I'd wear a tux to the ball. The seniors usually do. But if you'd rather I didn't—"

She turned back, knowing he could mean only one thing, but afraid of taking anything for granted. "Why should I mind?"

"I wasn't sure you'd want to go formal. And if I wear a tux you'd almost have to wear a party dress."

How impossible boys were . . . and how wonderful. "I have nothing against wearing a party dress," she said. "In fact, I'd love to."

Nothing could touch her happiness. It was a live thing inside her, pulsing, singing, rippling through her veins like a merry little brook. She bubbled, she tingled. She laughed at nothing. She and Ross were going to the Harvest Ball. If he'd still cared for Lela she was the girl he would have asked.

One day at noon Lela and Hank came up to the table where the decorating committee was having lunch, discussing the project while they ate. Lela wore a winter-white dress with a gold belt, and with her hair shimmering in a golden tide about her shoulders she was a dazzling sight. Hank looked down at her adoringly as she addressed Ross.

"I'm giving a party a week from Friday night," she said. "Hank has kindly offered to act as my host, but of course I want you to come."

Ross looked startled. "A week from Friday night? Why, that's the night of the Harvest Ball!"

"So what?"

"Who'll come to your party? Everyone will be at the dance."

Lela smiled. "No, they won't. I've already mentioned my party to several people, and most of them have said they'll come. It seems quite a few people prefer a private party, with no adult supervision, to a school affair. My parents are going to be away so we'll have the house to ourselves."

Ross jumped to his feet, eyes flashing. "Lela, you can't do this! I know the kids you'll ask, and we need them at the ball. Several of them are on committees, and the rest—well, they're the kind of people we need to make the affair really shine."

"I'm afraid that's just too bad." Lela idly toyed with one of the gold chains she always wore around her long neck, her taunting smile saying as plainly as words, This wouldn't have happened if you'd invited me to the ball. As she started to turn away she said, "Drop in if you like. It's open house."

Ross sounded as if he was choking. "Kate and I will be at the ball."

"That will be over shortly after midnight. My party will probably go on all night." Her eyes went to Kate. "Of course you're welcome to drop in, too—Kate."

Kate was beyond feeling hurt or insulted by the other girl's attitude toward her. It was Ross's reaction to Lela's announcement that she was giving a party the night of the Harvest Ball that disturbed her, made her feel sick all over. Was he so upset because he feared the dance would be a flop if Lela drew away a number of the top kids? Or was he worked up for a more personal reason? Perhaps the ball would mean nothing to him if Lela wasn't there.

"We won't be dropping in," he told the lavender-eyed girl whose taunting smile seemed to madden him. "And if you have any school spirit you'll cancel your party and come to the ball."

"Orange Grove, Orange Grove, rah, rah, rah!" Lela said, laughing. Then added, "Sorry, Ross, I'm afraid that's the extent of my school spirit."

Ross turned to Hank. "Maybe you can talk her out of this. We're using a football theme, and it won't mean a thing if you're not there."

The big halfback looked down at Lela, mutely appealing to her, but she merely tossed her head and said, "Come on. There are some more people I want to talk to. I want to invite as many as I can to my party before they buy their tickets to the so-called ball."

When the couple had walked away Ross sat down and pounded the table with an angry fist.

"Blast! You know what this is going to do, don't you?" he demanded of the group at the table. "An open house with plenty of free food and booze will practically wreck the Harvest Ball. I doubt if we'll sell enough tickets to pay expenses."

"I don't think it's that bad," Jaclyn said. "Sure, she'll get some kids, and some who would really add to the luster of the ball. Hank, for instance. Without him we may as well knock out the football theme. But we can play up Kate's idea and use oranges more extensively than we planned to. Maybe we can borrow some potted orange trees from Swenson's Nursery. They've helped us out in different ways in the past. We can place the potted trees all around the gym. Who'll volunteer to speak to Mr. Swenson? Kate, since using oranges was your idea—"

"Yes, sure I'll speak to Mr. Swenson," Kate said, but she could get little enthusiasm into her voice. Ross sat beside her, silent and grim-faced.

"Does anyone have any other suggestions?" Jaclyn asked.

"Why couldn't we have an orange juice fountain?" a girl named Nancy spoke up. "You know, like those champagne fountains they have at weddings. My sister was married last Sunday. That's what made me think of it," she explained.

"I'm glad you did think of it," Jaclyn said. "It's a great idea. Probably we can borrow one from some caterer. I'll ask around. To heck with those kids who'd rather go to Lela's party than to come to the Harvest Ball," she added.

Nancy laughed. "With the lushes all going to Lela's party maybe nobody will spike the punch this year. It would be nice if we could get by without that."

Ross turned on the girl. "Are you saying that only drunkards will go to Lela's party?"

Nancy, a rather shy girl, seemed to shrink within herself in the face of Ross's wrath. "No, of course not. I–I wouldn't have said anything if I'd thought—I mean, I didn't know that you and Lela were still—"

"Lela and I are friends," Ross said in a milder tone. "I'm disappointed in her that she'd do a thing like this, but I don't want to hear her slandered."

Jaclyn spoke up in an authoritative tone. "Let's finish our lunch before the bell rings."

Kate took a bite of tuna sandwich but found she couldn't swallow. She reached for her glass of milk, washed down the bite of food, but didn't try to eat any more. Ross, whose appetite was usually ravenous,

135

showed no interest at all in the food on his plate. Kate thought with a pang that there was nothing she could have done that would have affected him like Lela's announcement had. She thought again, as she had once before, that she and Hank were both pawns in a game of love that Ross and Lela were playing. They couldn't get along, yet they couldn't live without each other, either, so they did all they could to hurt each other. Ross had asked Kate to the ball; Lela had retaliated by planning a party the same night the ball would be held. She knew Ross would be miserable, stuck with a girl he didn't really care for, unable to even have the satisfaction of snubbing Lela, and dancing with Kate.

"You ready to go?" Ross said at last. Kate nodded, and he didn't comment, as he ordinarily would have done, on the fact that she hadn't eaten her lunch. How could he, when he hadn't eaten his own?

"It's sabotage," he muttered when they were in the hall. "She's trying to punish me for taking you to the ball."

"I'm sorry, Ross," Kate said in a small voice.

"Sorry for what?" he asked, giving her a sharp look.

"I don't know . . . sorry that you're so upset, I guess."

"You're not sorry you're going to the dance with me?" He stopped and looked at her, a new concern in his eyes. If she let him down at this late date he knew he couldn't get anyone the least bit attractive to go to the ball with him. Lela's triumph would be complete.

"Oh, no," Kate said. "How could I be sorry about that?" But she was, now that she knew he'd be with Lela that night, at least in spirit.

"I'll drive you home after school," he said, smiling his relief.

"You don't have to do that, Ross. I don't mind walking."

He swung her around by the shoulders. "What do you mean you don't mind walking? If you don't want me to give you a lift just say so, but don't go cold on me like this."

"I didn't mean to sound cold. And I *do* want you to drive me home." She looked up at him, hoping the tears that threatened her eyes didn't spill over. She could never please him for long, no matter how hard she tried. In fact, he was angry with her now because she *had* tried to please him, telling him he didn't need to drive her home.

He shook his head, all at once looking more baffled than angry. "Then why did you say you'd rather walk?"

"I didn't. I said I didn't *mind* walking."

He drew in a breath that expanded his big chest, then let it out in a mighty sigh. "My dad says there's no understanding women, and I guess he's right." His lips quirked in a smile now. "If you're *sure* you want me to drive you home, I'll wait for you in the parking lot after school."

If he was baffled, so was she. She talked it over with Doris that evening. Her friend came over after supper and they sat on the bed in her room as they had since they were little girls.

"Just think, we both have a date for the Harvest Ball," Doris said. "Me and Jeff, you and Ross. What are you going to wear?"

"I don't know," Kate said. "I almost wish I wasn't going."

Doris stared at her. "You're out of your mind. I mean, you've finally flipped."

"If you'll button up I'll tell you what I'm talking

137

about." She told Doris about Lela's party, and how Ross had reacted to the announcement. "He was— broken up. That's the only way I can think of to describe how he acted."

"Still, he asked you to the ball, so I don't see what your problem is."

"My problem is that I'm sure he'd rather go with Lela. He didn't ask her because they can't get along. They both have strong personalities that happen to clash. So they go with other people, but they're always trying to hurt each other. I think Ross likes me, in a way. If it weren't for Lela he might even love me, in time. But Lela's part of his life, and there's no way I can compete with her."

"Just the same, he wouldn't go with you if he preferred to be with her." But Doris's tone was not as positive as her words. She seemed to sense that people like Ross and Lela led more complicated lives than she and her friends. She quickly changed the subject to something she felt more comfortable with. "I'm going to look at dresses Saturday. I'm sure glad I have my babysitting money so I can buy something really nice. And I owe that to you. Thanks, Kate."

Kate waved away the thanks, but the fact that she'd been able to get jobs for Doris and so many other girls made her feel good.

"I guess I'll look at dresses Saturday, too," she said.

She went to Miss Smith's, the only place in town to go for a special dress.

"How is your lovely sister?" was the first question Miss Smith asked her. Anne had worked in the shop her last two years of high school.

"Anne is fine. She's going to Community College."

Only then did Miss Smith ask, "What can I do for you, Kate?"

"I need a dress for the Harvest Ball."

"You're going to the ball? How nice." The woman looked her over for size. "You're a ten, aren't you? I have some beautiful party dresses in your size. Gold is perfect for such an occasion, and it won't be too bad with your coloring. You have Anne's gray eyes, but you don't have her ash-blonde hair, do you?"

"No, I don't."

"Well, let's just try a few things on, and see how they look."

The gold dress looked fine, in spite of Kate not having Anne's blonde hair, and it fit perfectly, which surprised Miss Smith.

"Most girls are an inch too tall, or half an inch too short to wear a dress right off the rack. But you're just average size, aren't you?"

Kate's feet were average size, too. She had no trouble finding shoes which would be dyed to match the gown. Then there was the appointment to be made with the hairdresser.

"I'll want something special," she told the manager of the Belle Beauty Salon. "I guess you'd call it a high fashion set."

Here her ego got a boost. The woman ran a strand of her hair through her fingers. "You've got lovely hair," she said. "Plenty of body, yet silky-soft. And with that nice dark color we should be able to give you a set that will make your young man's eyes pop open."

Kate smiled, but she wasn't sure Ross would be impressed no matter how nice she looked. She could never be as stunning as Lela, with her golden hair and lavender eyes, her tall, willowy figure that made anything she wore look like high fashion. The whole evening would probably be a drag for him, with Lela entertaining so many of their mutual friends, the most sophisticated kids in school. *He'll be stuck with me and a bunch of other dull nobodys.*

13

The night of the ball would never come. So Kate would think one minute. The next she'd go into a panic because the day would be there before she could possibly get ready for it. She had a broken fingernail that simply must grow out, and she hadn't been able to find a wrap to go with the gold dress. What if she couldn't find a thing, and had to wear one of her old jackets? Her mother would never let her out of the house in November without some kind of wrap.

She hadn't much time to look, either. It was a busy social season, and the babysitting business was thriving. She mustn't neglect that, no matter what. . . . Then there was her work on the decorating committee.

"I guess that's it," Jaclyn said the day before the ball. "You've all done a great job. Orange Grove High thanks you. And a special thanks to you, Kate, for coming up with the idea of using oranges as our theme."

While Kate gave what she hoped was a gracious little bow, Ross, standing beside her, squeezed her hand.

"All set for tomorrow night?" he asked in an undertone.

She nodded, smiling up at him. No use telling him she still hadn't found a wrap. Man-like, he'd say, "Wear anything." They walked from the gym to the parking lot where all of a sudden the demons of self-doubt caught up with her. He smiled at her, he said the right words. But did he really want to take her to the Harvest Ball? With Lela not going he probably wouldn't go either if he hadn't already asked Kate before Lela sprang the news of her party.

"You're quiet," he said, as they cut across the parking lot.

She laughed a bit harshly. "People are always telling me that. If a girl isn't chattering every minute people seem to think there's something wrong with her."

He stopped and looked at her, a mixture of feelings reflected in his features. One brow was lifted questioningly, his eyes had a rather hurt look, while his mouth was set in a tight line. It was some time before he spoke, seconds in which Kate was certain she'd finally lost him with her weird behavior.

Then he said, quite gently, "I wasn't being critical, Kate. I just thought that if something was bothering you we might talk it over. Have I done something to offend you?"

She gazed up at him, loving everything about him right down to the last fading freckle on the bridge of his straight nose. No, you haven't done anything to offend me, she wanted to say. It isn't your fault you can't love me. She had an urge to release him from their date. If he were free of her he'd probably go to Lela's party.

"You could never offend me," she said softly. She might have said more, but he took both her hands in his and pressed them warmly.

142

"Believe me, if I ever did offend you it would be unintentional," he said huskily.

All of a sudden they were as close as if they were wrapped in each other's arms, there, in the middle of the parking lot, with shouting kids all around them, and cars spinning by, barely missing them. Then a small foreign car, bright yellow with black racing stripes, screeched to a stop beside them. Lela called to Ross from behind the wheel.

"Don't forget my party tomorrow night! Drop in after you feel you've done your duty by dear old Orange Grove High!"

She didn't wait for an answer, but gunned the powerful motor of the sports car and roared off.

Ross had dropped Kate's hand when Lela had driven up. Now he stared after the yellow car until it was out of sight. When he looked back at Kate his eyes were troubled.

"I wish she wasn't doing this," he said. "Word of the party is all over school. I'm afraid she's going to have trouble with crashers."

"It's open house, isn't it?" Kate challenged. "I don't think she'd have an open house if she didn't want a lot of people to show up."

"She wants her friends to come—not a lot of bums."

The way they stood glaring at each other it was hard to believe that a moment before they'd been holding hands, gazing tenderly into each other's eyes. The sight of Lela, a word from her, turned Ross into a different person.

Kate wished she could become a different person, too. Anne would not become flushed and angry because a boy preferred another girl, constantly defending her no matter how outrageous her behavior. *I'm not*

Anne. More and more she found it hard to adopt Anne's dignity, her gentle manner.

"If you're so worried about Lela why don't you go to her party?" she asked heatedly. "Don't let a little thing like a date with me stop you."

He stared at her. "I can't figure you out," he said, shaking his head. "We were getting along fine, and now—this."

As if it was her fault Lela had driven up, and he'd immediately started acting like a lovesick sophomore.

"You haven't answered my question," she said. "Do you want to skip our date and go to Lela's party?"

"It seems to me you're the one trying to get out of our date. Has someone else asked you—someone you'd rather go with?"

That was so comical she had to smile, and then it was no use trying to recapture her angry mood. She gave a titter, then his face broke into a grin, and the next minute they were laughing until there were tears in their eyes. When she could speak she said, "Well, John Travolta did call up and ask me to the ball, but I told him I already had a date."

This set them off again, and when they'd sobered once more he was the one who spoke.

"Funny how we have these little scraps. I guess the course of true love never did run smooth. Somebody said that—"

"Will," she said. "Good old Will."

Her heart was full and running over, full of love for Will Shakespeare, for everybody living or dead . . . most of all with love for Ross Barrows. *I guess the course of true love never did run smooth.* The words had been lightly spoken, and she mustn't take them too

144

seriously. Still, they were just about the sweetest words she'd ever heard.

When she got home Anne greeted her with the news that she'd found a wrap that might go with the gold dress. Anne, who made everybody else's problems her own had searched the shops around Community College at noon, and in a small boutique she'd found a stole.

"It's lying on your bed. If you don't like it I can take it back."

They both went to Kate's room. The stole was ivory-colored with gold threads running through it. They draped it around the gown and agreed that it wasn't perfect, but probably the best that could be found, gold being an impossible color to match, and not many colors going well with it that would be suitable for an evening wrap.

"Thanks, Anne! You're the most wonderful sister in the world!"

"How about me?" asked Carrie, who had just bounded into the room.

"You're wonderful, too!" As she gave Carrie a quick hug she told her that the little Fletcher boys could hardly wait for her to come babysitting.

"Wait till I tell Mom," Carrie said, round eyes bright. "If I'm old enough to be such a good babysitter, I'm old enough to date."

"I think you are, dear," Anne said. "I only hope Mom thinks so, too."

That night Mrs. Fleming put a platter of fried chicken on the table. "Dinner tonight is courtesy of the Colonel," she said. "I haven't got the hang of making those frames yet. When I do it will go faster, and I'll have more time for other things."

Mrs. LaCross had suggested that the needlepoint wall hangings would sell more readily, and bring a better price, if they were framed. Mrs. Fleming had at first declared she didn't know a thing about framing, and couldn't possibly learn. "I don't know which end of a tool to use." But with Kate's encouragement she'd bought the necessary tools and materials, and set up a little shop in a corner of the garage. She was more likely to be there these days than she was in the kitchen.

As the family ate the fried chicken and cole slaw, Carrie repeated the story Kate had told her about the little Fletcher boys looking forward to her sitting with them.

"That proves I'm grownup, doesn't it?" she demanded of her mother.

"Almost, I guess."

"Then I can walk to the movies with Doug, can't I?"

"Not just yet, dear." The mother seemed constantly absorbed with the cleanliness of her youngest child . . . a way of keeping her a baby? "Right now you'd better get a fresh napkin and wipe your face and hands," she said.

Poor Carrie. Kate didn't blame her for howling in rage. But at least Anne was happier than she'd been for some time. Larry had decided to come home for the Thanksgiving weekend, although it meant missing some work. Then shortly after that there'd be the Christmas holidays.

Friday night Kate's mother insisted that she sit down at the table and eat something, although Kate protested she'd choke if she tried to swallow a bite.

"You won't choke. In fact, you'll feel better after eating a little bit."

It was amazing how often mothers were right. Kate

ate a few bites, and some of the butterflies in her stomach quieted down. As soon as she was excused she hurried to her room where she'd already laid out everything she was going to wear. She'd even bought new, lacy underwear in a soft beige color, wanting to feel perfect from the skin out.

When she at last looked in the mirror she felt the way she thought a bride must feel on her wedding day—special, beautiful . . . touched with magic. Her dark hair had been arranged in a cap of soft curls. The gown molded her bustline, nipped her waist, and fell gracefully to the tops of her gold slippers. Anne had loaned her a gold chain with a floating heart, and when she'd pinned on the chrysanthemum corsage Ross had sent she was ready to go downstairs.

The family had hardly finished admiring her when she heard the Mustang drive up. When the doorbell rang Anne answered it, and brought Ross into the living room. Kate caught her breath at the sight of him. In a russet-colored tux, his hair carefully groomed, his dark-blue eyes glowing with a special light, he was as handsome as a movie star.

"Thank you for the beautiful corsage," Kate said.

He smiled. "The flowers aren't nearly as beautiful as you."

Carrie groaned at the extravagant compliment. Everyone else laughed lightly, then they were in the hall. Mrs. Fleming, who had followed them, kissed Kate on the cheek.

"Have a wonderful time, dear." Then to Ross, "Drive extra carefully, won't you? A lot of young people will be out tonight and there's bound to be some reckless driving."

"Don't worry, Mrs. Fleming. I'll take good care of Kate."

They laughed as they got in the car. "Parents!" Kate said. But she was pleased that her mother had made her little speech. Ross commented, as he had once before, on what a nice family she had.

The gym had been turned into a fairyland. Although she'd had a hand in the decorating, everything looked different at night. There were the colored lights playing over the scene, the young men and women all dressed up so that they looked older than they ordinarily did, and far more attractive. A full dance band added to the excitement, and there was the orange juice fountain on the refreshment table, a glamorous touch that Kate took personal pride in. If she hadn't suggested the theme of oranges, to honor the school name, most likely Nancy wouldn't have mentioned the fountain.

Ross was waiting for Kate when she came back from checking her wrap. When he held out his arms and she went into them, it was the happiest moment of her life. He lightly touched his cheek to hers as they danced the slow number. The bones in her body seemed to melt. She sniffed his shaving lotion, a clean, spicy aroma, and her knees went weak.

He must have felt the slight buckling, for his arm tightened around her. "Mind if I tell you again how beautiful you are?" he asked huskily.

She laughed softly. "I don't mind at all—after I've told you how handsome you are."

He moved back his head and grinned at her. "Glad you didn't come with John Travolta?"

"You bet. You're better looking than he is, and you dance better, too. Besides—"

"And besides I'm available?" he teased.

"No, that isn't what I was going to say." But now she was self-conscious and couldn't get out the words,

Besides, I love you. For one moment she'd been so full of her love for him she could have declared it without embarrassment. Then she'd realized she was Kate, and she wasn't sure enough of herself to tell him how she felt about him.

"What were you going to say?" he pressed.

"I can't remember now."

"Maybe you'll remember later." He held her closer. He knew what she'd been about to say, and he wanted to hear the words . . . but would he tell her that he loved her, too?

"Yes, maybe I'll remember later," she whispered.

The number ended, and he led her to the orange juice fountain. There were boisterous greetings as they found Tamara, Oren and Stan there. The boys wore dark suits, but Tamara was glamorous in a green strapless gown and full makeup. She was to sing "Shine on, Harvest Moon" at ten o'clock, just before the band broke for intermission. The old song was a tradition at the Harvest Ball.

"You look gorgeous," Tamara told Kate.

"So do you."

"Aren't Ross and Oren the lucky guys?" Tam asked with a laugh.

"I'll drink to that," Ross said, and raised his paper cup.

Stan, who was stagging it as usual, scoffed. "Toasts made in orange juice don't mean a thing. This is kid stuff. After Tam sings we're going to cut out and go to The Pump. You two guys, too. It wouldn't be complete without you."

He was talking to Kate and Ross. Before Kate's heart had a chance to sink Ross said, "No, not tonight, old buddy. I didn't rent a tux, and Kate didn't buy a new dress, so we could spend the evening in a beer joint." Belatedly, he looked at Kate. "You'd rather stay here, wouldn't you?"

She nodded, trying not to sound too eager as she said, "Ross is right. I want to get my money's worth out of this dress. I don't know when I'll ever wear it again."

"The girl has a point," Tamara said. "I didn't buy anything new or I'd probably feel the same way." She explained to Kate that she'd bought the green strapless dress for a singing engagement some time before.

The music started again, and Ross danced with Tamara while Kate danced with Oren. Stan led a pretty but shy junior onto the floor, probably giving her the thrill of her life. He boasted of not having a steady girl, but playing the field.

Kate was glad to be back in Ross's arms for the next dance, and the next. She felt as if she could dance forever and never get tired. Ross seemed to feel the same way. Sometimes they didn't even leave the floor when a number ended, but waited, holding hands, for the music to start again. . . .

Suddenly there was a fanfare and Tamara walked onto the stage, a spotlight following her as she crossed to the microphone. The dancers stood where they were while Tamara's full contralto voice rang out. She sang the verse of "Shine on, Harvest Moon," the theme song of the ball, then she invited everyone to join in the chorus. When the number ended she bowed, blew kisses to her wildly applauding audience, then disappeared into the wings. A few minutes later she and Oren danced close to Ross and Kate.

"We're cutting out after this dance," Oren said. "You kids join us out at The Pump if you get bored with this scene."

Ross shook his head. "Have fun out there, but we'll stay here. Right, Kate?"

"Right." She smiled up at him, thrilled that he'd rather be at the school dance with her than out at The Pump with his friends and fellow musicians.

It was some time later that he surprised her by missing a step and coming down on her toe. "Gosh, I'm sorry," he said. "I don't know how that happened. I—"

"Maybe you're tired. Let's sit down a while."

She expected an argument, but there was none. He immediately led the way to two empty chairs that stood against the wall. He crossed his long legs, and after a minute crossed them the other way. Kate looked at him, and realized, sickly, that he was bored. He looked out over the dance floor with blank eyes, and it was plain he no longer found the ball exciting. She could understand how he'd been stimulated at first, all dressed up in his rented tux, with her looking prettier than she ever had. The gym had seemed like an enchanted place, and even the younger, most ordinary kids had looked grownup and glamorous in their party clothes.

But soon the magic had started to fade. Even to her eyes the decorations now looked tawdry. The musicians were old, their music outdated. Most of the kids were dull, or too young to be interesting to Ross. Lela's party had drawn away many of his friends. Others, like Jaclyn, were school leaders and busy helping out the chaperones, seeing to the refreshments, and trying to get everyone to mix. For a while Tamara, Oren and Stan had added some fun to the evening, but with them gone there was no one left he cared about.

Not even me. If he really cared for me he wouldn't need anyone else.

"Do you want some more orange juice?" he asked after a while.

"No, thank you," she said politely.

151

It was awful. She wanted to run to the rest room and cry—or better yet, call her dad and ask him to come and get her. It was only ten-thirty. How could she stand this until midnight? How could he?

"I'll be back in a minute," she said at last. She'd go to the rest room, not to cry, but to give them a few minutes away from each other.

He nodded, and sprang up politely. All this politeness, when they'd been so close just a short time ago. *There's nothing worse in this world than someone you love being merely polite to you.*

She found Doris in the rest room. Flushed and breathless, she cried, "Isn't everything wonderful? The gym looks beautiful, and everyone is so dressed up you can hardly recognize them." She giggled. "Isn't it funny that we've been too busy to even say hello? Jeff doesn't want to miss a dance, and Ross has been keeping you busy, too, hasn't he?"

Kate smiled and nodded, as she got out her compact.

"Maybe the four of us can get together later," Doris said.

That's all Ross needs. "Sure," Kate said. "We'll look you up if we get a chance."

Her friend gave her a hurt look. She was young for her age in many ways, but she wasn't dumb. "Yes, do that," she said. She left the rest room with her head high, although Kate had seen the shimmer of tears in her eyes before she moved away.

Darn Ross. Why do I let him do this to me? But she knew the answer, and still hopeful that she might somehow rescue the evening, she carefully touched up her makeup, and rearranged a few curls that had fallen loose.

When she went back to the gym Ross was waiting for her. Taking her arm he said, "Let's get out of here."

"Where do you want to go—to The Pump?" If he did she'd go with him. She had no right to keep him away from his friends, to consider herself his girl if she was too straight-laced to go to a tavern with him and take a few sips of beer.

"No," he surprised her by saying. And then he dropped a real bombshell. "I thought we'd drop in on Lela's party."

14

They were outside before she found her voice. She came to an abrupt halt just outside the door that led to the parking lot.

"I don't want to go to Lela's party," she said.

He'd been moving so rapidly that he was two steps ahead of her before he could bring himself to a full stop. The moon was clouded over, but still she could see the tight lines in his face.

"What do you mean you don't want to go?"

"I mean just what I said. I don't want to go to Lela's party. I wasn't invited." Her voice didn't sound the way she wanted it to, firm and incisive. She sounded childish, aggrieved.

He moved back to her, again taking hold of her arm, this time squeezing it painfully. "You *were* invited," he said impatiently. "That day in the cafeteria."

"*You* were invited. The invitation to me was just an afterthought." She mimicked Lela's high-pitched voice. "Of course you're welcome to drop in, too— Kate." Her imitation of Lela was so good it boosted her

154

morale. In her own voice she said, "Let go of my arm. You're hurting me."

"I'm sorry." He released her arm, gave it a little pat as if to take the hurt away. "I know Lela hasn't been very nice to you," he said, "but that's because I've been dating you. She—sort of thinks I'm her property."

"And I sort of think she's right, or you wouldn't want to leave the Harvest Ball to go to her party." It was better to be sarcastic and angry than to reveal her despair. She was going to lose him. Tonight it was all going to end, the dream was going to die. If she refused to go to the party he'd be through with her. . . .

If she only had a good excuse not to go! But she didn't. It was early, so she couldn't plead that she had to get home. The only excuse she had was the one she'd offered, and he'd rejected it. She was in a no-win situation. If she refused to go to the party, which his heart was set on attending, he'd never forgive her. And if she went she'd be so out of place among his sophisticated friends that he'd be ashamed of her, know she was wrong for him. In the darkness of The Pump she might get by with taking just a sip of beer, but Lela's parties were famous for the heavy drinking everyone did. He'd expect her to go along, to get high, like everyone else.

"Please, Kate," he said, frankly begging now. "I'm really concerned about Lela. Hank is a good guy, but he can't handle some of those kids if they get out of line. If Mickey Darrow shows up there's bound to be trouble. I don't think you know him—he's a drop-out . . . every time he gets a few drinks under his belt he wants to fight someone. But I can handle him."

Oh, yes, Mickey. Lela and Ross had mentioned him some time ago. A drinker, a brawler. "I'm surprised you'd ask me to go to a party where you think there's likely to be trouble," Kate said. How priggish she sounded. She wouldn't have blamed Ross if he'd walked away and left her standing there. But he didn't.

"Most likely everything will be cool," he said. "I don't even know that Mickey will be there." He touched her arm, gently this time. "We don't have to stay long," he urged. "We can just put in an appearance. I'll see how things are going, and we can clear out—join the gang at The Pump."

Fine. Great. What were those two places that people got caught between? Oh, yes, Scylla and Charybdis. Or between a rock and a hard place, as her dad would put it.

"How about it, Kate?" His voice was soft, pleading. His fingers lightly stroked her arm.

She couldn't sustain her anger. She wanted with all her heart to please him, and she was near tears because she couldn't. "Please, Ross, don't ask me to go some place where I'm not wanted. Why don't you drop me at home and go on to Lela's?"

He dropped her arm as if he couldn't stand the touch of her. "And show up at the party alone? If I'd wanted to go stag tonight, I wouldn't have asked you out."

She didn't dare point out that he'd asked her to go to the Harvest Ball, not to a private party. Her armor was weak because she was lying about her reason for not wanting to go to the party. She could have put up with Lela's rudeness for a while. What she couldn't put up with was the drinking—either going along and drinking her share, or admitting she didn't drink which would prove to him she wasn't his kind of girl.

"Okay," she said at last, desperate for everything to be right between them again, if only for a little while.

"Thanks, Kate. I really appreciate it." He took her

hand and started across the parking lot, walking at such a brisk pace she could hardly keep up with him in her high heels. When they were in the car he tore out of the lot as if he was going to a fire. . . .

He drove silently toward Foothill Estates. Kate was silent, too, resigned. She had no plan of action. If she could get out of drinking she would, but if she couldn't —she just didn't know. She knew what her sisters would do. She knew what any number of other people would do, faced with a moral decision. But she was Kate, Kate the Unknown, an in-between girl who could go this way or that.

When they got to Ross's street he drove a few doors past his house, squeezed the Mustang in between two other cars in front of a large ranch-type house where there was obviously a party going on. The wide driveway was full of cars, and the blare of rock music could probably be heard a block away.

"It's a good thing we came," Ross said, jumping out of the car. "If she doesn't turn down that stereo the cops will be here in no time."

Kate climbed out of the car and followed him to the front door. He rang the doorbell, and when there was no immediate answer he threw the door open.

Ross sighed, "She doesn't even have sense enough to keep the door locked. Any kind of weirdo could walk right in." Before he closed the door he pushed a button, locking it.

Kate noted the luxury of the house in a detached sort of way. Big entrance hall with plank floors, richly furnished rooms opening off both sides. The music, loud talk and laughter came from farther back in the house. Kate wondered dumbly what she was doing there. Oh, yes, I'm here because Ross couldn't stay away, and didn't want to put in an appearance alone.

"I think I hear the doorbell!" Lela's high-pitched voice came from the back of the house. The next minute she was in the entrance hall. "Ross!" she cried, rushing forward. "I knew you'd come!" She threw her arms around his neck.

If anybody had told me I'd end this evening feeling tacky I'd have told him he was crazy, Kate thought. But tacky she felt in her stiff gold dress, and the stole that wasn't quite right with it. The toe of her slipper bore the imprint of Ross's shoe. She put a hand to her hair, confirming her suspicion that the cap of curls was now hanging like a mop. Lela was wearing a lovely Hawaiian hostess gown, low cut, in a splashy hibiscus print. She'd pinned a fresh hibiscus in her flowing golden hair. A shell necklace adorned her throat, and more shells jangled on her wrist. She moved in a cloud of White Ginger perfume as she stood back from Ross. She started to say something, but he spoke first.

"I found the door unlocked," he said in a stern voice. "I've warned you before how dangerous that is. And if you don't turn down that stereo you'll have the cops here for sure."

Lela laughed, throwing back her head. "You're always scolding me, but I know that's because you love me, so I forgive you. . . . Oh, I see you've brought your little friend—a—"

"A—Kate." Kate supplied the name herself, her voice surprisingly steady.

"I'm going to turn down the stereo," Ross said. He turned to Kate. "Lela will show you where to put your wrap."

He strode down the hall, disappeared from sight. Lela smiled at Kate, the smile of a cat with a cornered mouse. "Let's go to the bedroom, dear. I'm sure you want to get rid of that stole as soon as possible. I could have told you it's impossible to match gold . . . only mink or sable goes well with it."

"I prefer to leave fur to the animals it belongs to."

Lela laughed. "Oh, you're one of those—it figures. Ross has some funny notions, too, but he'll outgrow them. Sensible people do."

Sensible people don't run bait shops on the coast or tourist cabins in the desert, Kate thought. Maybe you're wrong about Ross. Maybe I am too, thinking he's in love with you. Maybe he's just concerned about you because you're an old friend.

She followed the other girl down the hall. They passed a large sunken room that appeared to be the family room. It was crowded with young people who were dancing or gathered around the bar. She recognized many of them as seniors from Orange Grove High. Ross stood by the stereo, adjusting the sound. Hank was by himself, over by a wall. He looked awkward and out of place, a can of beer in his hand, although he didn't seem to be drinking. Would he break training tonight. *And will I break my word to my parents?*

Lela opened a bedroom door. Kate tossed her stole on the bed, on top of a pile of wraps. Lela was right. She was glad to get rid of it.

"You'd better touch up your face," Lela said. "And your hair is a mess. You'll find makeup and hair spray on the dressing table."

"Thank you, but I have everything I need," Kate replied coolly. "Anyway, Ross and I won't be staying long. We just dropped in for a minute."

Lela gave a shrill laugh. *"We* just dropped in for a minute? Why not admit you didn't want to come at all, but that Ross insisted?" Before Kate could respond the girl's narrow features sharpened. "How stupid you are

159

if you think you can keep him away from me. There have been girls before, and there'll be girls again, because Ross is so attractive women won't leave him alone. But he'll always come back to me."

Kate was shocked, momentarily intimidated, by the fury of the other girl's attack. If she could only summon Anne's dignity, her sweetly aloof air—or if she could laugh and jibe like Carrie would do. Either of her sisters could make Lela Granger feel like two cents.

But she couldn't seem to slip into her sisters' personalities the way she used to. She was Kate, and though she wasn't sure just who or what that was, she found herself speaking with an authority that surprised her.

"You're awfully sure of yourself, aren't you? But you may get a big surprise one of these days. I don't think you know Ross at all."

"Ha! And I suppose you do?"

"This discussion is pointless. Let's just wait and see what happens."

Lela gave her a coldly measuring look that held a certain amount of respect, and flounced out of the room. Kate went to the dressing table, decided to do nothing to her makeup, which she'd touched up at the gym not too long ago. She repaired her curls the best she could, and sprayed them from a tiny can she carried in her bag. Not for anything in the world would she have touched any of the supplies on the dressing table.

When she left the bedroom she stood for a moment in the hall. If only she could drink a little wine or beer, get a little bit high so she could laugh and mix with the others, and make Ross proud of her.

Maybe I will, she thought. Why should it be so hard to break a promise she never should have made?

She started along the hall, walking hesitantly until she came to the wide archway of the family room.

When she reached it Ross spotted her and bounded up the half-dozen steps.

"I was beginning to think you were lost," he said. "Come join the party." He took her by the hand and led her down the broad stairs. "What do you want to drink?" he asked.

"What are you going to drink?"

"Beer. Wine gives me a headache."

"Okay, I'll have beer, too."

"I'll get ours from the fridge. The stuff at the bar is warm. Once you've had a couple you don't mind, but I like the first one ice-cold."

She withdrew to a corner. Nobody paid any attention to her. A space had been cleared in the center of the room, and some couples were dancing. Some lurched a bit as if they were half-drunk. Others were sober, or at least steady on their feet. She was sure Bridget and Ernie were sober. She knew them slightly, having sat at the same table with them in the school cafeteria. They were both friendly, and had struck up a conversation with her, although they were seniors and she was a lowly junior. Ernie was a slender, studious boy, Bridget a pretty dark-haired girl. As they danced close together, eyes half-closed they seemed to be off on a cloud, all by themselves.

Then suddenly a boy who'd plainly been drinking lurched up to them and tried to cut in. He was an older fellow, probably nineteen, tall and wiry with stringy light hair and pale eyes. He was shabbily dressed, in jeans and an old shirt, but from the expensive watch and gold chains he wore, Kate was certain he could have dressed better if he wanted to.

She couldn't hear what was said for the noise in the room, but the tall boy tapped Ernie on the shoulder, and Ernie shook his head. The older boy's face flushed and a dangerous glint came into his pale eyes. He gave Ernie a push, and tried to take Bridget in his arms.

"No!" she cried, fighting him off. "Leave us alone, Mickey!"

So the scruffily dressed boy with the stringy light hair was Mickey Darrow, who had a reputation for disrupting parties. . . . Kate held her breath as Ernie caught Mickey by the arm and tried to pull him away from Bridget. Everyone stopped dancing and stared, but no one tried to interfere. If there was a fight poor Ernie would get the worst of it. Kate was wondering if there was anything she could do when Ross charged into the room.

"Hey, cool it, Darrow!" he shouted. Hastily he handed the beer he carried to Kate, then got between the other two boys. He said a few words to Mickey in an undertone, and managed to coax him away from Ernie and Bridget. They, and the other couples, resumed dancing. Mickey drew a flask from his back pocket and took a swig. Evidently he wasn't satisfied with wine or beer, but had brought his own liquor. Ross frowned at him, said a few more words. From his expression Kate gathered he was warning Mickey to behave himself.

Ross was smiling by the time he reached Kate. "Sorry about that," he said, "but I think old Mick will settle down now."

Kate doubted it. She didn't know much about drinking, but she'd heard that alcohol turned some people mean, and she would have bet a bundle that Mickey was one of those.

She'd put the beer down on a table, a can and a glassful of the brew. Ross picked them up, and handed her the glass.

"I like mine right out of the can," he said, "but I figured you'd prefer a glass—right?"

"No," she said.

He cocked a brow quizzically. "You mean you'd rather have a can?"

"No. I—"

There was now a slight frown between his brows. "You want wine? Why didn't you say so?"

"I don't want wine or beer," Kate said. "I don't drink." She hadn't known she was going to speak the words until they were out.

His eyes searched her face, puzzled at first, and then angry. "You had beer at The Pump. You're just mad, aren't you, because I brought you here?"

"No," she said. "And I didn't drink beer at The Pump. I spilled it, if you remember. I know now that was silly. I should have told you the truth. You see, my sisters and I promised our parents we wouldn't drink until we're at least twenty-one."

It was amazing how easily the words came out once she'd started. Perhaps what was going on around her had something to do with it. Drunken talk and laughter, couples who were staggering as they tried to dance, Mickey swaying on his feet, a mean expression in his eyes—it all combined to make her feel rather proud of being sober and knowing she was going to stay that way.

But Ross—these were his friends, this was his way of life. He continued to look at her, frowning, silent, studying her as if she was something on a laboratory slide.

"Don't let me stop you," she told him. "Go ahead and drink your beer."

He seemed to have made up his mind about something—perhaps to make the best of a hopeless situation. "No," he said, "if you don't drink neither will I. People change when they drink, talk differently, act

163

differently. If I drink and you don't you'll be practically alone at the party."

"I don't mind."

"I do. I brought you here and it's up to me to see that you have a good time. Anyway, drinking is no big deal, at least not to me. I can take it or leave it alone."

She couldn't tell if he meant it, or if he was doing a good job of hiding his real feelings. Perhaps he was telling himself to go along with her tonight—he'd never be stuck with her again.

"Let's dance," he said. They were about to go into each other's arms when Lela came up. Her eyes were a bit glassy, but she slurred her words only a little bit when she addressed Kate.

"Would you help me in the kitchen a minute? I need some help with the refreshments and I remember how clever you were helping Ross's mother a while back."

"I'll help, too," Ross said, seemingly pleased that the two girls were getting along so well.

"No, men don't belong in the kitchen," Lela said. "You stay right here."

Kate followed her hostess, knowing she was walking into some kind of trap, but knowing there was no way out of it. When they reached the kitchen, where they were alone, Lela turned on her with a fury that shocked her.

"I want you to get out of here," she spat. "You're not only a wet blanket, refusing to take a drink, but you're keeping Ross from having a good time. I'll give you taxi fare if you'll go quietly, without saying anything to Ross."

Kate spoke coldly. "If I wanted to go home you wouldn't have to give me taxi fare."

"Oh, yes, I forgot. You're a big businesswoman . . . robbing little girls of their babysitting money."

Kate had never felt such rage. "If I leave the party—and I will if you don't apologize for that last remark—Ross will go with me," she choked.

"The heck he will! You couldn't get him away from here if you begged him on your knees."

"Want to put it to the test?" Kate challenged.

Lela hesitated, then snapped, "Forget it."

"I'll forget that, but I'm not forgetting your remark about my babysitting business. It isn't true, and I demand an apology."

Who was this girl, this Kate, who in the camp of the enemy dared to dictate terms, to demand an apology? And she'd pulled it off. She'd forced Lela Granger to say she was sorry.

"Well, I heard something like that at school. If it isn't true I—I apologize." She spoke stiffly, but then a pleading note came into her voice. "Just don't drag Ross away, will you? He's the only one who can handle Mickey if he gets in a fighting mood. And I don't dare get into trouble. The folks have threatened to make me finish the year in boarding school if I get in any more trouble."

For the first time Kate caught a glimpse of Lela as an insecure girl who desperately needed guidance and love. Instead of threatening to punish her why didn't her parents stay home and look after her? She acted like a woman of the world, but she was only seventeen. Kate remembered about her older sister, who'd run off and married in her teens, and never been home since. Would Lela go that route . . . perhaps with Ross?

"Ross and I will stay a while," Kate promised, although she didn't like the idea of Ross being called on to subdue a belligerent drunk.

"Thanks." Lela went to the sink and poured herself a glass of wine.

Back in the family room Kate found Ross stacking records on the stereo. He smiled at her. "I thought we'd have one more dance and hit the road."

She tried to read his expression, and couldn't. Did he want to leave because she was a wet blanket as Lela had called her, or had he had enough of the party?

He led her across the room toward the sliding·glass door that opened on the patio. The door was partly open, and the fresh air felt good. There was the scent of orange blossoms which Ross noticed at the same time she did.

"Orange blossoms," he said. "What does that remind you of?"

Her heart gave an erratic beat. He could mean only one thing. She turned her face up to his, a tremulous smile on her lips . . . then suddenly they both started as a commotion broke out behind them, a sound of scuffling, a boy's angry voice: "You stay away from Bridget!"

"Make me!" It was Mickey's voice. Kate swung around in time to see the older boy give Ernie a push that spun him around. Ernie staggered, tried to catch himself, but his momentum sent him flying in to the plate glass door.

"Don't, Mickey!" Lela screamed.

But her cry came too late, even if Mickey would have heeded it. The glass shattered. Ernie fell to the floor, blood pouring from a cut in his forehead. He was unconscious, eyes glazed.

15

There was pandemonium. Girls screamed. Boys shouted. Mickey, swaying on his feet, looked down at Ernie and shook his head, as if he couldn't understand why he was lying there. Bridget, who a few minutes ago had romantically clicked wine glasses with Ernie now stared down at him in shock, as a fluid, redder than wine, seeped from his forehead.

Lela screamed hysterically. "Look at the rug! My folks will kill me!"

Off-white carpet . . . very red blood. Hank pressed in the sides of an empty beer can he held, a befuddled expression on his face.

Why didn't somebody do something? Kate had hung back, feeling like an outsider, waiting for someone else to take over. Now she realized she was the only perfectly sober person in the house, the only one capable of acting. Except Ross. Where *was* Ross? He'd disappeared from her side . . . she looked around and saw that he'd gone for a towel. Hurrying back, he handed it to her.

"Press this against his forehead while I carry him to the car. We've got to get him to the emergency hospital in a hurry."

Her knees weak at the sight of the blood, her stomach turning over, Kate knelt and pressed the towel against the gaping wound. Ross got his arms under the slender boy, grunting as he lifted him. Nobody tried to help. Even Bridget was of no use to them for she had fainted soon after the shock had worn off. Nobody ran ahead to open the door. "My parents will kill me!" Lela was crying over and over.

"I just gave him a little push—nothing to hurt him," Mickey said in a complaining tone, the words heavily slurred.

Kate got the door open, trotted along beside Ross, to the car, managing to keep the towel pressed against Ernie's forehead. She climbed in the back seat, cradled Ernie's head in her lap. Ross, in a tight parking space, banged the front of the Mustang into the car ahead of him, then backed it into the car behind him. There was no time for careful maneuvering. Only One thing mattered. They must get Ernie to the hospital.

They were in the clear, racing toward Community Hospital, probably ten miles away. The towel was wet and sticky under Kate's fingers. She tried not to think of what the wetness was. She'd almost fainted once when her mother had cut her finger on a paring knife and bled just a little bit. . . .

"Ross, I–I think I'm going to faint, or–or be sick."

Driving frantically, without regard to stop signs or red lights, honking the horn at every intersection, Ross didn't hear her weak cry.

"Where are the cops, now that I need them?" he groaned. "I'd give anything for a police escort!

She was glad he hadn't heard her. She was going to be all right. Suddenly she'd made up her mind to that. She wasn't going to faint, and she wasn't going to be sick.

"How's he doing?" Ross called out.

Her fingers probed, and she said, "I think the worst of the bleeding has stopped."

"His pulse?"

She hadn't thought of that. Maybe the bleeding had stopped too late. She felt the slender wrist and a faint but steady beat pulsed against her fingers.

"It seems pretty steady."

"Good. Just hold on, Kate. We're almost there." He gave a hoarse chuckle. "I'm sure glad you're not one of those fainting women."

"Faint? Me?" She laughed, too, slightly hysterical now that the worst of it was over.

Ernie stirred at last, groaned, and opened his eyes.

"Where am I? What's going on?"

He tried to sit up, but Kate pushed his head back onto her lap. "You fell in to the plate glass window at Lela's, and got a pretty nasty cut on your head. Ross and I are taking you to Community Hospital. We'll be there in a few seconds."

"I remember now," Ernie said, although he spoke fuzzily. "Mickey was coming on to Bridget. I got into a scuffle with him, and he pushed me in to the door. Darn roughneck." Kate remained silent and he went on, "It was my fault, though. Bridget wanted to go to the Harvest Ball, but I was proud of being invited to Lela's party and talked Bridget in to going there, instead. That's not my league, though, and I know it now."

"Hush, you're talking too much." The flow of blood had started up again. Worried, she'd just begun to apply fresh pressure when Ross shot into the brightly

169

lighted emergency entrance of the hospital. He leaned on the horn, and had no sooner screeched to a stop when a door opened and two white-clad figures ran out, a man and a woman.

"What seems to be the matter?" the woman asked. Before Kate could answer she peered in to the back seat and saw the boy, who had lapsed into unconsciousness again. "Get a gurney," she ordered the man.

When Ernie had been placed on the rolling stretcher the woman spoke to Ross. "I'm Dr. Gomez. I want you and the young lady to come inside. You'll have to answer some questions."

"Okay," Ross said. He got out of the car, helped Kate out. Following some distance behind the doctor who was helping push the gurney, they held hands like frightened children. "He'll be all right, Kate."

"Sure, he'll be fine, Ross. He has to."

"Gosh, if I'd had any idea the evening would end like this—" His voice trembled, faltered, then he took a sighing breath and went on, "I'm sorry, Kate."

"It's all right," Kate said, squeezing his hand. She was weak from reaction, but she had to hold up, for Ross's sake.

When they reached the emergency room, Ernie was being wheeled into a treatment room. A nurse motioned them to come to the desk. She asked them to give their names, also Ernie's, and to tell where, and how, the accident had happened. When Ross had given his name and address Kate gave hers, and then supplied the rest of the information. She didn't mention the drinking, and made as little of the scuffle as she dared.

"Where does Ernie live?" the nurse asked.

"I don't know," Kate said. When Ross shook his head she got up. "He probably has some ID on him. His parents have to be notified."

She went into the treatment room, came back with an ID card.

"How is he?" Kate asked.

"He'll require quite a few stitches." She dialed a number. "Mr. Bennett? Your son Ernie has had an accident. He's in the emergency room at Community Hospital. . . . We'll have to stitch closed the gash in his forehead." The connection was broken, the nurse hung up, and spoke to Ross. "You two can run along now. You did fine, getting him here as soon as you could."

"I'll take you home," Ross told Kate, "then come back and stay till we know he's okay. Maybe he'll need blood."

"I have blood, too," Kate said.

The nurse spoke up. "Thanks, kids. I don't think it'll come to that, but I'll let the doctor know if it does. You can sit on the bench over there."

Sitting on the bench Ross reached for Kate's hand. His face was pale as he bent his head to hers. She thought he was going to apologize again for taking her to a party she hadn't wanted to attend, a party that had ended like this. She'd tell him he wasn't to blame himself, that she'd made the decision to go. . . .

"I sure hope Lela doesn't get into trouble over this," he said hoarsely. "If her folks put her into a boarding school instead of letting her finish high school at Orange Grove I don't know what will happen to her. In the kind of school they're threatening her with she'd be practically a prisoner. Thanks for not mentioning the drinking, Kate."

Kate carefully withdrew her hand. How foolish she'd been to think Ross's concern was for her. He always seemed to think of Lela first.

They both jumped up as Dr. Gomez came out of the treatment room. "How is he?" Ross asked.

171

The dark-skinned young doctor looked tired, drained. "He'll be all right, thanks to you." She gave a little nod. "Nice work."

Ross took Kate's arm. "Let's go."

She needed no urging. Maybe, just maybe, her parents wouldn't have to know about this. It was almost one o'clock. They'd be in bed, although her mother would still be awake. "I'm home, Mom!" she'd call, and hurry to her room.

"Thank heaven Ernie is going to be okay," Ross said as he put her in the car. "I just hope you don't get into trouble with your parents. I know they wouldn't approve of you going to a party like that."

"I'm not going to tell them if I can help it."

Ross had no sooner backed out of the parking place than another car raced in from the street and shot into the space. A couple jumped out and ran for the emergency door.

"Probably Ernie's parents," Ross said.

"Yes."

Ross drove toward her house in silence. They were halfway there before he burst out, "I'm sorry about this whole evening, Kate. You didn't want to go to the party, but I—"

"Please, Ross," she said wearily, "let's not hash it over."

He seemed satisfied to let it go at that. When they reached her house he left the motor running.

"I know you're in a hurry to get in. And I want to get back to Lela's as soon as I can. Maybe if we can get all traces of blood out of the carpet her parents won't have to know there was any trouble."

Of course he wanted to go to Lela. It was always Lela.

"Good night, Ross," she said. He started to bend his face toward hers, but she turned away and opened the car door. She wanted no more kisses from him, not even a polite good night kiss.

The porch light was on, also a light in the living room. If her mother was up she was ruined, her dress stained with blood. She couldn't wrap the stole around her because she'd left it at Lela's. Her hair was a mess. She felt it hanging in strings around her face. She'd have to explain that this had happened at a party she'd gone to when she was supposed to be at the Harvest Ball—a *drinking* party.

"Mom?" she called softly from the hall. There was no answer. Gratefully, she stepped to the living room and switched off the light. She tiptoed to the back of the house. "Mom?" she called again. She heard her father's rhythmic snores. Then her mother's low voice.

"How was the ball, dear?"

"Fine." She manufactured a noisy yawn. "I'll tell you all about it in the morning."

"All right, Kate. Have a good night's sleep."

She thought of Macbeth as she washed the gold-colored dress in the bathtub. She ran the water carefully so as not to wake Anne. She didn't have to worry about Carrie, who slept like the dead. At last the dress was clean to Kate's satisfaction. She blotted it in a thick bath towel to remove the excess moisture, so she could hang it in her closet.

As she climbed into bed at last she promised herself, I won't think. I'll just go to sleep. She was so tired she ached all over. She closed her eyes, breathed deeply, and felt herself grow drowsy. Just before sleep came she murmured, "Good night, Ross—and good-bye."

16

Kate groaned when the telephone rang on Saturday morning. She'd wanted to sleep late, to put off thinking of the night before, and the problem she might have if the family questioned her too closely.

"Hello." Then belatedly, "Kate's Dependable Baby-sitting Service." Most likely anyone calling her at nine o'clock on Saturday morning was calling for a sitter.

It was Mrs. Parsons, who had a complaint. Fern Nelder had sat for her the night before.

"I asked her to do the dinner dishes, but when we got home they were still in the sink," she said in an outraged tone.

"Did you offer to pay her extra to wash the dishes, Mrs. Parsons?"

"No, of course not. She had nothing else to do all evening. Certainly my little boys are no problem. So why couldn't she—"

"Your little boys are a handful, Mrs. Parsons. That's why some of my girls refuse to sit with them. And my sitters are not cleaning women."

"I don't like your attitude, young lady, and I don't intend to use your service again."

She hung up before Kate could say, "That suits me fine." The call made Kate glad she'd started her service. *No one takes advantage of my girls.*

She looked at the rumpled bed, wishing she could go back to sleep and sleep at least until noon. She dreaded facing the family. They'd want to know all about the Harvest Ball. She wouldn't lie, no matter what. *I'll just answer very, very carefully.*

She couldn't go back to bed. She smelled bacon and coffee, and Carrie's shrill voice came from the kitchen. "I want waffles! You make pancakes all the time. Why can't we have waffles at least once in a hundred years?"

Kate washed, brushed out the bedraggled curls, got into jeans and her coral-colored sweater. Saturday morning she usually went to the table in her robe, but this morning she felt more comfortable being dressed. If the questioning got on dangerous ground she could jump up from the table and say she had to run to the store. Since she'd had her business she sometimes had to run out for supplies.

Her mother had catered to her youngest daughter's appetite, as usual, and made waffles.

"Here's one all ready for you, sleepy-head," Mrs. Fleming greeted Kate.

Her dad put aside his paper. "Well, how was the dance?" he asked. "I bet you were the belle of the ball."

Kate managed a laugh as she buttered a waffle. "Not exactly, but—I had plenty of dances."

"Did everyone like your dress?" her mother asked, pouring fresh coffee for her husband and herself.

"Yes, I got lots of compliments."

Anne said, "I bet you were thrilled when everyone sang Harvest Moon."

Kate nodded. She thought Anne looked pale, and forgot her own problem for a moment as she questioned her older sister. "Don't you feel well, Anne?"

Mrs. Fleming answered the question. "Anne had a disappointment last night. Larry called and said he won't get home for Thanksgiving, after all."

"Oh, Anne, I'm sorry!" Kate cried.

Anne smiled wanly, and cut a bite of waffle, although she didn't raise it to her mouth.

Carrie finished her second waffle, and gulped down her milk. "Hey, Kate, did you go any place after the dance?" she asked.

Kate's heart dropped with a thud. But then her mother saved the day—or at least the moment.

"You have a milk moustache, Carrie. For goodness sake, wipe it off. A white moustache isn't very becoming on a little girl."

"I'm not a little girl! And I know when to wipe my mouth!"

"Then why don't you wipe it?"

By the time the familiar argument had run its course Kate knew she was safe. Chances were the subject of the ball wouldn't come up again. She pushed back her chair.

"I'll do the dishes, so the rest of you just go about your business. I know you want to get to your framing, Mom."

"Why, yes, I have another one of my florals ready for—"

The telephone rang. "I'll get it," Mrs. Fleming said, "although it's probably for one of you girls." She stepped into the hall.

Mr. Fleming sipped his coffee and read the sports

page, grumbling about the Rams. Carrie had decided to scrape the last of the batter into the waffle iron. Anne insisted on helping Kate with the dishes.

"Okay, but I'll wash," Kate said. She'd just plunged her hands into the soapy water when her mother came back into the kitchen.

"Kate," she said quietly, but there was a note in her voice that made Kate's heart feel as if it had dropped into the pit of her stomach.

"Yes, Mom?" She turned around, wiping her wet hands on her jeans.

Her mother's face looked frozen. "That was Mrs. Bennett," she said. "It seems her son Ernie was badly cut at a party last night. She wanted me to tell you how grateful she and Mr. Bennett are that you helped get their son to the hospital."

"What's this all about, Kate?" her father asked, pushing aside his coffee cup, placing the folded paper beside it. "You were at the Harvest Ball, weren't you? Could this woman have you mixed up with someone else?"

While her parents and sisters stared at her, Kate shook her head. "No, she didn't have me mixed up with anyone else." In a few words she told it all. . . . Ross had wanted to go to Lela's party. There'd been drinking, a scuffle, Ernie had been pushed in to a plate glass door. She and Ross had rushed him to the hospital.

"You were *drinking?*" her mother asked, eyes blank with shock.

"No, of course not. Neither was Ross, but I guess all the others were."

"How come you went to a party at Lela Granger's?" Carrie spoke up. "Everybody knows the kind of parties she gives."

177

"Is that true, Kate?" Mrs. Fleming asked. "Did you go there knowing there'd be drinking?"

"Yes." It was a time for simple truthfulness, no evasions, no excuses.

Her mother sighed heavily. "Well, Kate, it seems your father and I don't know you at all. How many times when we've thought you were at the movies, or a school affair, have you been at a wild party? And how can I believe that you haven't broken your promise to us? How could you run with such a crowd, and not drink?"

"That isn't fair, Mother! I've never lied to you!"

"Didn't you lie just a little while ago when you told us about the ball, all smiles, no mention of cutting out and going to a party?"

Mr. Fleming spoke up. "She didn't actually lie, dear, so let's not accuse her of that. She was willing to deceive us, though, and she showed very poor judgment in going to a party like that. I'd suggest we give her a little time to think it over. How about grounding her for two weeks? I'd make it longer if she hadn't helped get that boy to the hospital."

Mrs. Fleming heard her husband out, then turned to Kate. "You heard your father. You're grounded for two weeks."

Kate felt a curious satisfaction. It seemed she had always got by without punishment. Her mother was usually too involved with Anne or Carrie to make much of her wrongdoings.

"Thanks, Mom, for not going harder on me." Impulsively, she ran and threw her arms around her mother's neck. Her mother seemed surprised.

"Well, it's hard to punish a heroine, and that's what you are if you helped someone else. But, there, don't cry."

She *was* crying, though, but it was all right because her mother's arms were hugging her. Her mother stroked her hair, kissed her wet cheeks.

"You'd better go lie down for a while. You're usually my self-contained one, but this has been too much for you. I imagine the worst part was keeping it to yourself. You should have told me last night. I would have scolded you, but parents have that right—just as you youngsters have a right to make mistakes."

So that's what I am, Kate thought—self-contained. She snuffled, gave her mom a last hug, dropped a kiss on her dad's tiny bald spot, and went to her room. Limp with relief that the worst had happened, and the sky hadn't fallen, she welcomed the idea of lying down for a while.

She'd just kicked off her sneakers when there was a knock on the door . . . Carrie's imperious knock. "Come in!" she called.

When the door opened both her sisters came in. Carrie's eyes were round with curiosity. Anne, too, seemed eager to hear more about the night before.

"Tell us all about it," Carrie prompted, making herself comfortable on the foot of the bed. "I'll probably never go to a wild party, and I'm sure Anne won't. Is Lela's house real super?"

They all sat on the bed, as they had when they were little girls. Kate didn't mind answering the question about Lela's house, but she hoped she wouldn't be quizzed about the accident. It was something she didn't want to live over.

"I guess you could say her house is super. It's big, and sort of luxurious."

"What did the kids do—" Carrie snickered— "besides drinking?"

"They danced, ate snacks, stood around and talked. Just like people do at any party."

"Wasn't there any adult supervision?" Anne asked. When Kate shook her head her older sister said, "It's no wonder Lela gets into trouble. The wrong kind of kids naturally gravitate toward a place where they think they can get by with anything."

"That's right," Carrie said. "And I think you were dumb to go there, Kate. You could get a bad reputation that way."

Kate threw a pillow at her sister, who threw it back.

"Hey, stop it, you two," Anne said. "This is no time for a pillow fight. Mom wants you to rest, Kate." She got up from the bed. "Come on, little one."

"Don't you dare call me that!" Carrie flared up. "It's bad enough that Dad does, and that Mom treats me like a baby, and always will." She got to her feet, and hands on her hips, she glared at her oldest sister.

"I didn't mean to upset you, honey," Anne said. "I mean Carrie. Mom does baby you, and I guess I do, too, but I didn't know you minded so much."

"Well, I do. How would you like to be treated like an infant all your life? Even when I'm twenty Mom will be wiping my chin."

Anne smiled gently. "I guess that's what you get for being the youngest, just like I've had to toe the mark because I'm the oldest. Ever since the day Kate was born, and when you came along even more so, I had to set a good example for you. 'You wouldn't want one of your sisters to do that, would you?' Mom would ask if I wanted to do anything the least bit questionable. Even now, at nineteen, I can't spend a weekend in the same town with my fiancé because it might give you girls ideas." She looked at Kate. "I don't think you know how lucky you've been, never having to shoulder the responsibility of being the oldest, and never being treated like a baby, except when you were a baby."

"Me—lucky?" Kate gasped. "I thought I was—" She started to say "neglected," then changed it to, "I just thought I was sort of blah, being the middle girl."

They all smiled at each other, sisters who suddenly understood each other better than they ever had. As Anne and Carrie started to the door Kate spoke.

"Carrie, did you ever stop to think that you've helped Mom make a baby of you? I mean, if you'd talk to her, tell her how you feel, instead of pouting, she might take you more seriously. You might also start acting like a young lady. She'd have no excuse to wipe your chin if you weren't always spilling something on it."

Carrie's round eyes grew thoughtful. A moment later she dashed from the room. "Mother, I want to have a serious talk with you!" she called in a newly mature voice.

Anne laughed softly. "I hope it works for her. You were so right in what you said, Kate. She's been playing the role the folks cast her in."

"Yes, and she's not the only one." Kate looked levelly at her older sister. Anne looked back at her, startled.

"Oh, no!" she said. "You don't mean—"

"Yes, I do. There are planes leaving for San Francisco every hour, even more around Thanksgiving."

"But Mom would be so hurt if I wasn't here and Dad would be so disappointed—" She broke off, laughed nervously. "I know what that sounds like, but it's hard to break a habit you've had all your life. I'll think about it, though."

"Yes, you do that. Now I'm going to lie down for a while. I do feel kind of knocked out."

Anne nodded. "Yes, you lie down and have a nice rest."

Kate hadn't slept much the night before, but had no idea she'd sleep now. She'd just relax, think over all that had happened—

The next thing she knew there was a knock on the door.

"Are you coming out for lunch?" Anne called, "or shall I bring you a tray?"

"Be right there!"

Marveling that she'd slept the morning away, Kate quickly jumped up, washed, brushed her hair, stepped into her scruffy sneakers and hurried to the kitchen.

"All I've made is sandwiches," Mrs. Fleming said. "If anyone wants a salad, or anything else, they can make it themselves. I'm anxious to get to my framing." She sounded a little wistful as she added, "With you girls almost grown up now—even Carrie—it's a good thing I have something to turn to, something I really enjoy."

Carrie slathered mustard on her sandwich, as usual, but she ate carefully, frequently wiping her chin.

Again the family was about to leave the table when there was an interruption. This time the doorbell rang. Mrs. Fleming, who was already up, said she'd get it. In a moment she was back.

"It's Ross," she told Kate. "I didn't tell him you were grounded. I'll leave that to you. You may see him for ten minutes."

Ten minutes was more than enough time to settle things between them, Kate thought. Perhaps Ross was there to tell her he wouldn't be dating her anymore, perhaps not. Maybe he thought they could go on the way they had been, but she knew that wouldn't do.

They had to reach some kind of understanding. She couldn't go on liking him when she wasn't sure of his feelings for her. The time had come for him to choose between Lela and her.

He stood in the hall. He must have been a bit pale because his eyes looked darker than usual, and the freckles seemed to stand out on the bridge of his straight nose. He was dressed in worn jeans, and an old brown shirt, but he looked, oh, so handsome, so appealing, it was all she could do not to run and throw her arms around him.

Controlling the impulse she said, "Hi. I've been grounded because of last night, but we have ten minutes. Shall we sit in the car?"

As they walked to the car he told her that Mrs. Bennett had called to thank him. "She said she'd called your house and talked to your mother. Knowing how your parents would most likely feel about you going to a party like that I figured you were probably in trouble. I'm sure sorry, Kate."

"It's not your fault. I went to the party voluntarily."

"Still, if I'd known you didn't drink—"

"That's not your fault, either. I should have told you right off the bat."

They were in the car now. "Why *didn't* you tell me?" he asked.

"I guess I was ashamed of being different—unsophisticated. I kept thinking I'd drink a little beer or wine if I had to. But, like I told you, I promised my folks I wouldn't drink, at least until I'm twenty-one, and when it came right down to it I couldn't break my promise."

"Of course you couldn't. If you were the kind of girl who could break a solemn promise I wouldn't feel the way I do about you."

"How *do* you feel about me?" She looked at him soberly, chin slightly tilted, knowing she was strong enough to accept his answer, no matter what it was. *Just be honest with me.*

His expression was as serious as hers. "I like you a lot," he said. "Only sometimes you've confused me. I mean, you've seemed like different people at different times . . . sometimes so dignified, other times clowning and cutting up. But when you're really *you,* like you are now, natural and sincere, I like you more than I've ever liked any girl."

He *liked* her. She'd never really doubted that. It was the love that was one-sided. She smiled, accepting the answer as she'd promised herself she would.

"I think I'll be really me from now on," she said. "Between last night and today—well, I've learned a lot about myself."

He smiled back at her and reached for her hands. "How long are you grounded? There are lots of things coming up during the holidays. I hope we can go to some of them together."

"Two weeks," she said. "But, Ross, I'm not sure I'll be going with you even when the two weeks is up."

He squeezed her hands. "You're mad about last night!"

"No, I'm not."

He didn't release her hands, but looked at her, eyes puzzled, questioning, hurt.

Was it worthwhile to speak her mind? You couldn't demand that someone love you, and she wouldn't even want to. Yet he had a right to know why she wasn't sure she'd be going out with him when she was free to date again.

"I know you like me," she said. "But you seem to love Lela. You asked me once if I was going with anyone else. I told you no. But you've never told me you weren't going with anyone else."

She withdrew her hands, looked away. She was glad she'd gotten the words out, but still her cheeks burned with embarrassment.

"I haven't been going out with anyone else!" he declared. "I—have a certain feeling for Lela, but I haven't been dating her."

She looked back at him, indignant now, thinking of the ball last night, how he couldn't wait to get away, go to Lela's party . . . all the times that Lela had come between them.

"I don't care if you call it dating, or what," she said, "but she dominates your life. Last night was an example. You were so bored at the dance I felt as if you were a million miles away from me. Only you weren't that far away, were you? Just as far as Lela's house."

He looked dazed, as if she were suddenly speaking a foreign language. "Bored? I wasn't bored, Kate. But I was worried about Lela, and the more I thought about her having open house without anyone to keep a lid on things the more worried I got. After a while, I just had to check things out."

"Why should you worry about her? What makes her your responsibility? That's what parents are for, isn't it?"

"Not the kind of parents she has. They've always neglected her, and they neglected her sister, too. The two little girls used to come over to my house, crying from loneliness. My folks did what they could for them, and I sort of adopted Lela, because she was the youngest one. For a while I thought I was in love with her, but that was before I met you. I don't love her, Kate—I just feel protective toward her."

She weighed what he'd told her. He wouldn't be Ross if he didn't feel compassion for someone who was lonely and neglected. This part of his nature was one of the things she loved about him, although, ironically, Lela considered it a weakness. Still, she concluded, compassion was one thing—an eighteen-year-old boy assuming responsibility for a seventeen-year-old girl was something else. She couldn't afford to become more deeply involved with Ross if he was going to continue to let Lela manipulate him, keep him in hot water all the time. She'd never be able to count on him, would become a part of an unwholesome triangle.

"I'm sorry, Ross," she said, "but as long as you feel that Lela is your responsibility, I think we'd better not see each other. Perhaps you do love her. Maybe you're mistaking love for pity."

"No!" His eyes flashed, then immediately softened. "I love you, Kate."

The words she'd longed to hear. They went straight to her heart, piercingly sweet, words she'd treasure forever.

"I've loved you for a long time," she said.

He reached out his arms and grasped her shoulders. "I know what you've been trying to tell me Kate. Lela isn't my responsibility. Anyway, I think her folks will do something now. My mother intends to give them a good talking to. Lela's sister had a baby a few months ago, and it looks as if her marriage is going to work.

Maybe Lela can stay with her." He reached for her again. "So let's not talk about Lela anymore. Let's talk about us."

She couldn't have resisted the pleading in his eyes even if she'd wanted to. She went into his outstretched arms, their lips met and clung in the longest kiss they'd ever shared. When they broke apart at last they just looked at each other for a while, smiling, taking a loving inventory of each other's features. Then Kate broke away.

"I've only got a couple of minutes left," she said. "Do you know how Hank is? He was drinking last night."

"I know. He was in such bad shape when I got back to Lela's that I drove him home. I stopped at a 7-11 on the way and poured some coffee into him, so his folks wouldn't see him that way. When he began to sober up he was one sorry fullback. I don't think he'll ever break training again. An athletic scholarship means too much to him. Incidentally, he's decided he doesn't belong with Lela and her crowd."

Kate nodded. "I have to go in now. And remember, Ross, we can't talk on the phone and no dates for two weeks."

"I understand." He grinned, then gave Kate one last kiss on her cheek before she opened the car door and ran up the path.

"See you, Kate!" Ross called after her.

She laughed, thinking of how that parting had worried her in the past. Not anymore. "I love you," he'd said. *And I love you.*

They might love each other for the next six months, or the next year. Maybe they'd love each other forever. They were too young to be sure. She might decide to go on to college, study child psychology. Ross had no idea of what he wanted to do.

He'd told her she'd confused him. I was confused, too, Ross, she thought. I wasn't sure who or what I was. But now I know myself, at least a little bit better. And she knew as time passed, she would find out even more.

If you enjoyed
this book...

...you will enjoy a *First Love* from Silhouette subscription even more. It will bring you each new title, as soon as it is published every month, delivered right to your door.

Filled with the challenges, excitement and anticipation that make first love oh, so wonderful, *First Love* romances are new and different. Every *First Love* romance is an original novel—never before published—and all written by leading authors.

If you enjoyed this book, treat yourself, or some friend, to a one-year subscription to these romantic originals. We'll ship two NEW $1.75 romances each month, a total of 24 books a year. So send in your coupon now. **There's nothing quite as special as a First Love.**

First Love from Silhouette

NEW BOY IN TOWN
Sixteen-year-old Stacey Hippner loves her parents but she resents their restrictions—especially when they involve Garr Garwin, the new boy in town.

KATE HERSELF
Kate Fleming had always felt the insignificant middle sister. That was before Ross Barrow, the most popular boy in school asked her out.

PLEASE LET ME IN
Melissa Johnson had always dreamed of being in with the most popular crowd. When Greg Scott, hero of the high school football team, begins to date her, she feels she has really made it.

FLOWERS FOR LISA
Lisa Kelly's interest in flowers earns her a summer job at Rick Brewster's father's florist shop. She is thrilled when she and Rick start dating. But she wonders if their relationship will turn out to be only a summer romance.

GIRL IN THE ROUGH
Kate's life as the brainy big sister of adorable, popular Mimi was not easy. When Kate took up golf all this changed.

First Love from Silhouette

THERE'S NOTHING
QUITE AS SPECIAL AS A
<u>FIRST LOVE.</u>